There was a man by the edge of the roof with a rifle.

His back was to Clint, who had to haul himself the rest of the way up as quietly as he could. He didn't count on the rooftop being covered with gravel. As soon as his boots touched the rooftop, the gravel crunched beneath his feet.

The man with the rifle whirled and Clint had no choice. As the rifle barrel came around, he drew and fired. His bullet struck the man in the chest. The rifle flew from his hands and off the roof, and the man followed. The bullet had shoved him back against the parapet, and he flipped over. He must have been dead already, though, because he made no noise as he fell . . .

DON'T MISS THESE
ALL-ACTION WESTERN SERIES
FROM THE BERKLEY PUBLISHING GROUP

THE GUNSMITH by J. R. Roberts
Clint Adams was a legend among lawmen, outlaws, and ladies. They called him . . . the Gunsmith.

LONGARM by Tabor Evans
The popular long-running series about Deputy U.S. Marshal Custis Long—his life, his loves, his fight for justice.

SLOCUM by Jake Logan
Today's longest-running action Western. John Slocum rides a deadly trail of hot blood and cold steel.

BUSHWHACKERS by B. J. Lanagan
An action-packed series by the creators of Longarm! The rousing adventures of the most brutal gang of cutthroats ever assembled—Quantrill's Raiders.

DIAMONDBACK by Guy Brewer
Dex Yancey is Diamondback, a Southern gentleman turned con man when his brother cheats him out of the family fortune. Ladies love him. Gamblers hate him. But nobody pulls one over on Dex . . .

WILDGUN by Jack Hanson
The blazing adventures of mountain man Will Barlow—from the creators of Longarm!

TEXAS TRACKER by Tom Calhoun
J.T. Law: the most relentless—and dangerous—manhunter in all Texas. Where sheriffs and posses fail, he's the best man to bring in the most vicious outlaws—for a price.

THE GUNSMITH

346

LADY EIGHT BALL

J. R. ROBERTS

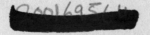

JOVE BOOKS, NEW YORK

THE BERKLEY PUBLISHING GROUP
Published by the Penguin Group
Penguin Group (USA) Inc.
375 Hudson Street, New York, New York 10014, USA
Penguin Group (Canada), 90 Eglinton Avenue East, Suite 700, Toronto, Ontario M4P 2Y3, Canada
(a division of Pearson Penguin Canada Inc.)
Penguin Books Ltd., 80 Strand, London WC2R 0RL, England
Penguin Group Ireland, 25 St. Stephen's Green, Dublin 2, Ireland (a division of Penguin Books Ltd.)
Penguin Group (Australia), 250 Camberwell Road, Camberwell, Victoria 3124, Australia
(a division of Pearson Australia Group Pty. Ltd.)
Penguin Books India Pvt. Ltd., 11 Community Centre, Panchsheel Park, New Delhi—110 017, India
Penguin Group (NZ), 67 Apollo Drive, Rosedale, North Shore 0632, New Zealand
(a division of Pearson New Zealand Ltd.)
Penguin Books (South Africa) (Pty.) Ltd., 24 Sturdee Avenue, Rosebank, Johannesburg 2196,
South Africa

Penguin Books Ltd., Registered Offices: 80 Strand, London WC2R 0RL, England

This is a work of fiction. Names, characters, places, and incidents either are the product of the author's imagination or are used fictitiously, and any resemblance to actual persons, living or dead, business establishments, events, or locales is entirely coincidental.

LADY EIGHT BALL

A Jove Book / published by arrangement with the author

PRINTING HISTORY
Jove edition / October 2010

Copyright © 2010 by Robert J. Randisi.
Cover illustration by Sergio Giovine.

ISBN: 978-0-515-14849-7

JOVE®
Jove Books are published by The Berkley Publishing Group,
a division of Penguin Group (USA) Inc.,
375 Hudson Street, New York, New York 10014.
JOVE® is a registered trademark of Penguin Group (USA) Inc.
The "J" design is a trademark of Penguin Group (USA) Inc.

PRINTED IN THE UNITED STATES OF AMERICA

10 9 8 7 6 5 4 3 2 1

ONE

"Do you play pool?"

"What?"

"Pool," Jerry Sacks said. "Billiards. Do you play?"

"I have played," Clint said. "Why?"

Sacks handed Clint his predinner brandy and said, "Come with me."

Jerry Sacks had a ranch just outside Tucson, Arizona. He had sent an invitation to Clint to come and stay awhile. To sweeten the invitation, he offered Clint five hundred dollars to "come and listen to a proposition."

Clint assumed the proposition was about to be broached.

He followed Sacks from his office, down a hallway to another room, which was dominated by a green felt-covered table.

"Pool," Sacks said, pointing to the table.

"Very nice," Clint said. It reminded him of the table that was in the pool parlor where Morgan Earp had been killed in Tombstone.

"Let me see you shoot," Sacks said.

"Jerry," Clint said, "what's going on?"

"Humor me," Sacks said, "please."

Sacks was in his fifties, had worked hard for what he had. When he became rich, he became a gambler—with money, not with his life, or his future. He'd finished gambling with those, because he had won.

Clint assumed this had something to do with Sacks's new status as a gambler.

There was a rack of pool cues on the wall. Clint went over and chose one.

"Wait," Sacks said. "Roll it on the table."

Clint had seen men do this, to see if the cue was warped. It never mattered much to him, but he did as Sacks asked. Rolled it, found it warped, took another, did the same, was satisfied with it.

"Shoot some balls," Sacks said.

The balls were already deployed around the table, as if a game had been interrupted, only none of them had been sunk yet.

Clint chose a ball, shot, sank it. Picked another, sank that one, too. Then he tried a combination and missed.

"See? I'm an amateur," Clint said.

"But you saw that shot," Sacks said, "set it, you just rushed the play. See, I've got a theory that the same skill that makes you a dead shot would make you a good pool player. In fact, a great pool player."

"And this is important why?"

Before he could answer, Sack's younger wife, Julia, appeared at the door.

"Dinner is served, gentlemen," she said. "Jerry, you're not supposed to be shooting pool."

"I'm not, dear," Sacks said, "Clint is."

"Well, come and eat," she said. "You can continue doing what you're doing afterward."

"We better go and eat," Sacks said. "Otherwise she gets testy."

Clint returned the cue stick to the wall rack and followed Sacks from the room.

"What's going on, Jerry?" he asked as they walked to the dining room.

"I don't have time to tell you now," Jerry said, keeping his voice low. "After dinner we'll go back into the pool room for cigars and brandy. I'll tell you all about it then."

Clint touched Jerry's arm, stopping him before they were out of the hallway.

"How about my five hundred?"

"Now?"

"I have the feeling I've been brought here under false pretenses," Clint said. "I'd like to at least get that money up front."

"I don't have that much in my pockets," Jerry said. "We'd have to go to my office. If we do that, we'll be late to dinner and I'll never hear the end of it. Gimme a break, Clint."

"After dinner, then?"

"Right after dinner."

"Before we talk about pool," Clint said.

Jerry Sacks nodded.

"Before we talk about pool."

"Okay, then," Clint said. "Lead the way."

TWO

Dinner was just the three of them—Sacks, his wife, and Clint. He had known Jerry Sacks for over ten years, but this was the first time he was meeting his wife. Sacks and Julia had married only four months ago.

"Is the steak to your liking, Clint?" she asked.

"It's excellent," Clint said.

Julia was in her thirties, almost twenty years younger than her husband. As Clint understood it, they had met in San Francisco and she had come back with him to be married.

"Good," she said. "We have a new cook. I was hoping you'd like it."

"Everything is great."

"Jerry told me you like peach pie," she said. "I had the cook make one for you."

"That sounds great," Clint said. "I appreciate it."

Something was wrong, but he couldn't put his finger

on it. Julia felt wrong to him. But he doubted that had anything to do with what Sacks wanted to talk about.

Julia cleared the plates away herself and brought in a tray with coffee and peach pie.

"Wow," Clint said after a bite, "my compliments to the cook. This pie is great."

"Well," Sacks said, "I guess her job is safe for a while, then."

Julia gave her husband a sharp look.

"We've gone through a few cooks in the last few months," he told Clint.

"I'm only trying to make sure we get the best we can," Julia said.

"I know that, honey," Sacks said. "I know it."

"Coffee's good, too," Clint said, filling in the awkward moment."Clint and me are gonna go and have a cigar," Sacks told Julia.

"No pool for you, Jerry," Julia said. "Doctor's orders."

"I know, Julia. I know. Come on, Clint."

Clint nodded to Julia and followed Sacks back to the room with the pool table. Sacks closed the door behind them.

"Doctor's orders?" Clint asked. "Is she serious? Or was that some kind of code?"

"No, she's serious. I hurt my back a while ago. Wanna laugh? I fell down those damn front steps, in front of the house."

"Can't tell by the way you're walking."

"Walking, standing, sitting, it's all okay," Sacks said. "But bending over, that's the problem."

"Like leaning over a pool table?"

"Exactly."

Clint walked to the rack, took down the same cue stick he'd used before.

"So what's on your mind, Jerry?" He leaned over, stroked a ball into a pocket. Easy shot.

"You play poker, right?"

"Right."

"High stakes?"

"Sometimes."

"With men like Bat Masterson? Luke Short?"

"That's right."

"Well, I'm a shit poker player," Sacks said, "but I'm a hell of a pool player."

"Where's this taking us, Jerry?"

"I've got a high-stakes pool match in two weeks," Jerry said. "I've already made a deposit, which I can't get back, and I'm not going to be in any shape to play."

Clint shot a ball into a pocket, then put the fat end of the stick on the floor.

"Wait a minute," he said. "Is this where you ask me to play for you?"

"You can do it," Sacks said. "We've got two weeks to get you good enough."

"You're crazy."

"No, I'm not," Sacks said.

"Don't you have someone else?" Clint asked. "Somebody who already knows how to play?"

"No," Sacks said, "I want you."

"Why?"

"I've got a few reasons. Want to hear them?"

"I want to hear them all," Clint said, "but first my five hundred."

"You're a hard man," Sacks said. "Wait here."

Sacks left the room, presumably to go to his office for the money. When he came back, he closed the door again, then handed Clint five hundred dollars.

"Thanks," Clint said. "I'm ready to hear the reasons now."

"Well, first, I trust you. Second, if I try to get somebody else, somebody who already plays, word will get around."

"And?"

"Well . . . it'll affect the side bets."

"There's open betting?"

"As well as a pot."

"What's the pot?"

"Each man has put in twenty thousand."

"How many players?"

"Ten."

Clint whistled.

"Two hundred thousand?"

"And plenty more in side action."

"Where's the match?"

"Right here in Tucson."

"That's convenient."

"Not so much," Sacks said. "It's my baby. I put it together."

"Must be killing you that you can't play."

"More than you know."

"What's in it for me?" Clint asked.

"Twenty percent."

"Is it winner take all?"

"Yup."

"So we're talking twenty thousand?"

"That's right."

"And you're willing to risk it all on me?"

"You've got the eye, Clint. And the heart."

"Yeah, for guns or cards."

"No, for this, too," Sacks said. "I can feel it."

Clint thought a moment.

"Will you do it?"

"I tell you what," Clint said. "I'll give you a week. If by then you don't think I can do it, you'll have time to find somebody else."

"I won't need anybody else," Sacks said. "But if that's the way you want it, agreed."

The two men shook hands.

"Here," Clint said, holding out the five hundred.

"Keep it," Sacks said. "Bet it on yourself. Or hedge your bet and play against yourself. Your choice."

"If I bet it on myself and win, do I split that with you, too?"

"No," Sacks said, "that'll be yours."

"When do we start the lessons?"

"Tonight," Sacks said. "In fact, right now. Rack 'em."

THREE

The plan was for Clint to stay at the house while he learned what he had to learn from Sacks. He had a room upstairs, took all his meals with Sacks and Julia.

Clint still felt that Julia was wrong, and it appeared to him that she felt the same about him. He caught her looking at him from time to time, and when she realized she was caught, she'd smile an insincere smile. He had the feeling she didn't like him—maybe because he was seeing right through her.

She liked living in the big house, and having the money, but Clint felt she didn't love Sacks at all. But he was no expert, so he tried to ignore his own feelings. He also tried to ignore the fact that she didn't want him there. Sacks was his friend, and he did want him there. On top of that, he needed him there.

The lessons started every day after breakfast, broke for lunch, started again, and then dinner. After that, Clint was on his own. If he wanted to go into town, he could.

He went in a couple of nights a week, just to refresh

himself. He ate, had a beer at one of the saloons, played some low-stakes poker, and returned to the house. He was determined to give Sacks his best, and to that end avoided any distractions—like women.

At the end of a week he and Sacks were in the pool room. He shot for two hours under Sack's watchful eye, then leaned the stick on the floor and looked at his friend.

"It's been a week," he said.

"I know."

"So?"

"So what?"

"What do you think?" Clint asked. "Should we continue with this?"

"You want my honest opinion?"

"What else would I want?" Clint asked.

Sacks hesitated, then said, "I think you have the best eye, the best hands, and the best instincts I've ever seen. You could be the best there is at this game."

"That's the truth?"

"The whole truth."

Clint looked at the table.

"Well," he said, "I thought I was doing pretty good, but . . ."

"I said you *could* be the best," Sacks said. "It would take a lot more practice. More than another week."

"What about your match?" Clint asked. "Do you want to find somebody else?"

"Oh, no," Sacks said, "I think you could win the match."

"But . . . there'll be better players there."

"Does the best player at the table always win in poker?"

"No."

"Who does?"

"The player who gets hot."

"That could be you," Sacks said. "You've got a good eye for combinations, but you rush your play. Take your time, take a deep breath. Also, you're not sure when to hit it hard and when to finesse the shot."

"Will you be at the match?"

"Oh, yes."

"Then you can signal me when to hit hard and when not to."

"I suppose I could," Sacks said.

"A nod for hard, a stroke of your jaw for short. Is that cheating?"

"It's coaching from the sidelines," Sacks said. "I don't know of any rule against it."

"There's no rule in poker either," Clint said, "but it could get you killed."

"You'll have your gun."

"I can wear my gun during the match?"

"I don't see why not," Sacks said.

"Well, this is your match, right?" Clint asked. "You make the rules?"

"I suppose that's true."

"Then with another week you think I'll be ready?"

Now it was Sacks's turn to give it some thought.

"Let's say I can't think of anyone else I'd have a better shot with."

"Well," Clint said, "that's faint praise, but I guess I'll take it."

"Faint?" Sacks asked. "There's a lot of money riding on this, you know."

"That reminds me."

"What?"

"Should I bet the five hundred on myself?"

"I'll let you know when the time comes."

FOUR

Three days before the match, Sacks had to go into town to start making arrangements.

"I've got to set up rooms for the players, food and drink, the works," he said. "You want to come?"

"No," Clint said, "I think I'll get in some more practice."

"Good man. I'll be back later this evening."

"See you then."

Later in the afternoon, while Clint was still shooting, Julia came into the room. That is, she stopped at the doorway, leaned against the door, and watched.

"I understand you're pretty good," she said.

He hadn't seen her since breakfast. She had been wearing a dress then, but now she had on a shirt, which was tucked into tightly fitting jeans, cinched at the waist.

"That's what Jerry tells me."

"Well, he should know," she said. "He's got a lot of money wrapped up in this match of his."

"So he tells me."

He stroked a ball into the corner pocket, and she came deeper into the room.

"You know," she said, "I don't understand this game."

"Really?" he asked. "Jerry hasn't taught it to you?"

She smiled and said, "It's not one of the things we do together."

"It's very easy," he said. "You just have to hit the colored balls into the hole, but you have to use the white balls to do it."

"Any ball? In any order? What about the numbers on them?"

"Well, yes, in some games they have to be hit in order."

"What about the game you'll be playing?"

"Yeah, the game we'll be playing I'll have to put them in the holes in order."

"Well," she said, leaning on the table and looking at the setup, "doesn't look that hard." She looked at him. "Can I try?"

"Sure."

He went to the rack and picked out a stick, handed it to her.

"How do I hold it?" she asked.

"Come around to this side of the table," he said.

She obeyed. She was wearing a scent so subtle he hadn't detected it until now. She got right in front of him and leaned over the table.

"Like this?"

She wasn't holding it right, so he leaned over her, their bodies touching.

"Like this," he said, redirecting her hands.

"Oh."

The scent was in her hair. Shampoo? He couldn't tell. Maybe something else. Something deliberate? She was his friend's wife—his much younger wife.

"No, draw the stick back, and then hit the white ball."

She did so, and her cue tip slid off the ball so that it skittered to one side.

"Okay," she said, "maybe it's not so easy."

She stood up, pressed herself against him. She was tall. She pushed her firm butt against his crotch, felt him react.

"Ooh," she said.

"Julia . . ." he said warningly.

"What?"

She moved her butt against him.

"You're a beautiful woman . . ." he said.

"Thank you."

"But you're married."

"He's not here."

"I know, but he's still your husband, and my friend."

She turned to face him, and now her full breasts were pressed against his chest.

"He's my much older husband," she said.

"He's not so old," Clint said. "What . . . fifty?"

"Fifty-six," she said. "Over twenty years older than I am. Do you know what that means?"

"That you married him for his money?"

If he thought she would be insulted, he was mistaken. She chuckled, a sound that sent shivers up and down his spine.

"Well, yes," she said, "but it also means that I'm not a satisfied wife—in the bedroom, I mean. And Jerry seems to think that you are quite a hit with the ladies."

"Is that what he said?"

"Among other things."

Clint wondered what the other things were. He didn't like the situation he was in. Why would Sacks tell Julia stories about Clint and women, and then leave them alone in the house? Was this a test? And if so, who was testing him, Sacks or Julia?

Clint backed up, but Julia stayed with him. Then she turned and walked away, crossing to the other side of the table.

"This isn't going to happen, Julia," he said.

"Coward." She said it with a smile. "What if I take off all my clothes?"

"Then you'll be naked in an empty room."

She chuckled again.

"All right, take it easy," she said. She walked to the rack on the wall and replaced the stick. "I was just playing."

She walked past him and, as she left the room, said, "Supper will be on in an hour."

"I'll be there."

He'd caught a glimpse of her face just before she left the room. Was the look on her face one of disappointment?

FIVE

Clint practiced hard for the last three days before the match was to start. There were no more tests from either Julia or Jerry Sacks.

At breakfast that morning Jerry said, "We'll be moving into the Alhambra Hotel, and staying there 'til the match is over."

"All the other players staying there, too?" Clint asked.

"That's right," Jerry said. "Everything will be taking place in that building."

"Sounds like it's going to be pretty close in that building."

"Don't worry," Jerry said, "it's a big building."

"What about you, Julia?" Clint asked. "You going to come and watch the match?"

"I might drop in from time to time," she said, "if just to make sure my old fool doesn't try to play."

"Don't worry about that," Jerry said. "My back's still a mess, and I've got Clint to do my shooting for me."

"And how is his shooting?" Julia asked.

"This boy's got the potential to be the best player I ever saw," Jerry said.

"I just want to be good enough to win this match for you, Jerry," Clint said. "I'm not looking to become the best. Poker is still my game."

"And there'll probably be a poker game or two going on in the building as well," Jerry said.

"Any rules against me playing in both?" Clint asked.

"As long as one doesn't interfere with the other," Jerry said.

"Sounds like there might be a profit to be made all around."

"You sound pretty confident, Clint," Julia said. "Are you always this confident?"

"Just when it comes to the things I'm good at, Julia," Clint said.

"And I'll bet there are a lot of them, huh?"

"Right now we're only concerned with one," Jerry said, interrupting their banter without noticing it. "Pool. You ready, boy?"

"Ready as I'll ever be," Clint said.

"Let's go, then," Jerry said, standing up. "The players will be arriving today and I want to introduce you."

"See you later, Julia," Clint said as her husband went out of the room.

"Count on it," she said to Clint in a low voice.

Clint and Jerry rode into town and went directly to the Alhambra, which had its own livery stable.

"Clint, this is Aloysius," Jerry said, introducing Clint to the black liveryman. "Everybody just calls him Al. He'll take care of your horse."

"Can you handle him?" Clint asked the man.

"Mr. Adams, I been handlin' horses all mah life," the man said, "and dat's more'n seventy years."

"Well, okay, Al," Clint said, handing over the reins, "but be careful with him. He's bitten off a lot of fingers in his time."

"Don't worry, Mr. Adams," Al said, "me an' dis here big fella's gon' get along jes' fine."

"I'll bet you will."

Clint followed Jerry into the hotel. They bypassed the front desk, the clerk and Jerry exchanging a nod. They went upstairs, down a hall, and Jerry stuck a key in a door and swung it open.

"Your suite," he said, holding the key out to Clint.

"A suite?"

"As befits the man representing me," Jerry said.

Clint entered a two-room suite as opulent as anything he'd seen in San Francisco—but on a smaller scale.

"What about the others?" Clint asked.

"Regular rooms," Jerry said, "but they're all very nice."

"I mean, when do they get here?"

Jerry took his watch from his pocket and checked it.

"The stage arrives in half an hour," he said. "The train a half hour after that. Unless somebody's ridden in already, they'll all be coming in then."

"What do we do until then?" Clint asked.

"I have to check out the rooms," Jerry said. "The pool room, the poker room—"

"Poker room?"

"I told you there'd be poker."

"You made it sound like there'd be some pickup poker games," Clint said. "Do you mean there's an official poker game? With prize money?"

"Well, winner-take-all money," Jerry said.

"Why didn't you tell me about that one?" Clint asked.

"Because I knew you'd want to play in that one, and I need you for the pool match."

"You tricked me."

"I didn't trick you, I . . . misinformed you."

"Same thing."

"Clint, the money's not as big in the poker game as it is in the pool game—especially not with the side bets. You stand to make a lot more money."

"Well," Clint said, "if I lose early, I can join the poker game, right?"

"Jesus," Jerry said, looking stricken, "don't even kid about that."

"Okay, then," Clint said, "let's go and look at your table."

SIX

The table looked the same as any other table to Clint. Green felt top, same number of pockets.

To Jerry, however, it must have looked like the Holy Grail.

"Beautiful," Jerry said, running his hand along the felt like it was a woman's smooth, silky skin.

"What about these cues?" Clint asked, looking at all the sticks hanging on the wall in a rack.

"I brought all this stuff in from Chicago," Jerry said. "Cost me quite a bit. This was all made by Brunswick."

"How much is a bit?"

"Not so much that we won't make a profit when we win," Jerry said, "but winning is about more than just the money."

"What's it about?"

"It's about being the best," Jerry said. "You know all about that, Clint."

"In poker," Clint said, "being the best means you won the most money."

"Right," Jerry said, "the money is how you keep score." He took his watch out again. "We better meet that stage."

Five players got off the stage. All were unknown to Clint. He wondered who were the pool players, and who were the poker players. They all complained about the ride, how crowded and bumpy it was.

Jerry had to see to their needs, which left Clint alone in the lobby with only the desk clerk.

Clint walked over. The man looked up at him. His hair was slicked; he wore a pin-striped suit and a bowtie, looked to be in his mid-thirties.

"Can I help you, Mr. Adams?"

"Any other players check in?" Clint asked. "Somebody who may have ridden in on their own?"

"I believe several players rode in on their own and checked in, sir," the clerk said. "Two yesterday."

"What were their names?"

The clerk opened the register and read off three names. None were familiar to Clint. How could there be a big poker game in the wind and no recognizable names coming in to play? Maybe they'd be coming in on the later arriving train.

It occurred to him that he didn't know the stakes of the poker game. All he knew was that Jerry told him he'd make more money playing pool. Maybe the stakes weren't high enough to attract players the caliber of Bat Masterson and Luke Short.

"Okay," Clint said, "thanks."

"Will you tell Mr. Sacks?" the clerk asked. "I meant to, but . . ."

"I'll pass the word on," Clint promised.

"Thank you, sir."

"If you see him first, though," Clint said, "tell him I'll meet him at the train station."

"Yes, sir," the clerk said, although he clearly hoped Clint would see Sacks before he did.

SEVEN

Clint heard the train whistle at the same time he saw Jerry Sacks appear on the platform. Jerry waved a hand and joined him.

"Did you see the clerk at the hotel?" Clint asked.

"No," Jerry said.

"He told me three others had ridden in and checked in on their own."

"Hmm," Jerry said. "I'll see who they are later."

The train came into view.

"Do you know who's arriving by train?" Clint asked.

"I have an idea."

"I'm curious about this poker game you're hosting," Clint said.

"What about it?"

"So far," Clint said, "there don't seem to be any well-known players competing."

"What does that matter?" Jerry asked. "As long as there are players."

"What are the stakes?"

"There's a winner-take-all pot of twenty-five thousand."

"Put up by who?"

"By me."

"That's not a lot," Clint said, "considering what we're playing pool for."

"The poker game is incidental," Jerry said. "The pool game is the main thing."

The train pulled into the station and came to a stop. A conductor jumped off and set down a step for the passengers to use when disembarking.

As the passengers came, Clint and Jerry moved closer. A man stepped down, wearing a top hat.

"Gentleman Lou Teacher," Jerry said. "One of the finest pool players in the country."

Behind him came a second man, wearing an ill-fitting brown suit, no hat, the sun causing his bald head to gleam.

"Cue Ball Wilson," Jerry said, "called that for obvious reasons."

"Any good?" Clint asked. "Or just colorful?"

"He's good," Jerry said, "if he can hold his temper."

Next, a woman stepped off the train. The conductor extended a hand to aid her, and she accepted it. She had long hair the color of copper, and a full figure tucked into a green traveling suit.

"Who is that?"

"That," Jerry said, "is Lady Eight Ball."

Clint looked at him.

"You're kidding."

"Do I make fun of poker player names?" Jerry asked. "Three-Fingered Harry? Straight Flush Freddie?"

"Hey," Clint said, "Harry does only have three fingers on his right hand."

"Well," Jerry said, "Antonia is a lady."

"Her name's Antonia?"

"Antonia Delaware."

"Oh, now I know you're kidding," Clint said.

Several others got down from the train, with Jerry reeling off their names, but he said the only ones Clint had to worry about were Gentlemen Lou and Antonia.

"She's a pool player?"

"One of the best."

"This could be interesting, then."

"Come on," Jerry said, "let's make our presence known and take them over to the hotel."

When they arrived at the hotel, Jerry got busy showing all the players to their rooms. Clint noticed Antonia tossing him a glance as she followed Jerry up the stairs. She hadn't said anything but hello when they were introduced, but the look on her face said she recognized his name.

Left to his own devices for the moment, Clint stepped out of the hotel lobby and walked over to the saloon. It wasn't busy and he got a beer quickly from the bored-looking bartender.

"Here for the game?" the barman asked.

"That's right."

"Lotta money to play for."

"Guess it is."

"Poker or pool?"

"My game is usually poker, but this time it's pool," Clint said.

"New to the game, then?"

"As anything but a casual player, yeah," Clint said. "You play?"

"From time to time."

"Not this week?"

"No," the bartender said. "this week I'm just the bartender."

"What's your name?"

"Danny Troy." The man stuck out his hand.

"Clint Adams." Clint shook it.

"The Gunsmith?" Danny asked. "I never heard nothin' about you playin' pool."

"I think that's the general idea."

"I see."

"You know any of these players?" Clint asked, and then listed some of the names.

Danny said he did, and proceeded to give Clint some tips on playing each of them.

"And you mind a little piece of advice?" he finished.

"Not at all."

"Use a heavy stick when you break," Danny said. "Gives you added power. Then switch to a lighter stick for finesse."

"Thanks," Clint said. "I'll keep that in mind."

"And one other thing."

"What's that?"

"Fast Eddie's in this match," Danny said. "Heard he's already in the hotel. Watch out for him. He's your biggest competition."

"Thanks, Danny."

"'Nother beer? On the house."

"Why not?"

EIGHT

Clint remained in the bar, talking with Danny Troy, until Jerry Sacks showed up to collect him.

"We're meeting in the pool room to go over a few things," he said.

"Okay," Clint said. He finished the beer and pushed the mug over to Danny. "Thanks for the beer, and the advice."

Out in the lobby Jerry asked, "What advice?"

"Danny plays pool, so he gave me some pointers."

Jerry put his hand on Clint's arm to stop him.

"What kind of pointers?"

"Just a few words about each of the players," Clint said, "and a warning about a character named Fast Eddie."

"Fast Eddie's one of the ones who came in on their own," Jerry said. "And he is somebody you should watch out for. Come on. I'll introduce you to him."

As they entered the room, Clint saw the players assembled around the table. Lady Eight Ball had changed into a blue dress with a plunging neckline. Clint wondered if she played in that kind of outfit—or if she was allowed to.

"Some of you know each other," Jerry said, "but none of you know this fella as a pool player. His name is Clint Adams."

"Adams?" Cue Ball said. "What the hell's he doin' here?"

"I'm not as rude," Antonia said, "but I'm wondering the same thing."

"He's playing in the match," Jerry said, "in place of me."

"Why aren't you playin'?" Gentleman Lou asked.

"Bad back," Jerry said.

"So he's playing in place of you?" Lou asked.

"That's right," Jerry said, looking around the table. "Anybody got a problem with that, speak up now."

"Hey," Cue Ball said, "I got no problem playin' pool against a gunmen."

He laughed, and some of the other players joined in.

"As long as you're backing him with your money," Gentleman Lou said, "I've got no problem."

"As long as he don't shoot the balls into the holes," another man said, "I don't have a problem either."

"That," Jerry said, pointing to the man who had just spoken, "is Fast Eddie."

Eddie, a slender, handsome man in his thirties with startling blue eyes, bowed his head slightly.

"Just Fast Eddie?" Clint asked.

"That's all the name I need," Eddie said.

"You can all get acquainted, or reacquainted, after we go over a few ground rules."

"Oh, good," Antonia said, "rules."

"Everybody ready to listen up?" Jerry asked.

"We're ready, Sacks," Cue Ball said, "but talk slow so's we can all understand you."

"Cue Ball," Jerry said, "I'll lay this out so even you can understand it."

The man scowled. Clint figured he could dish it out, but he couldn't take it.

NINE

The rules were fairly simple and nobody seemed to have any problems following them. When Jerry was done, he said, "There are some back rooms downstairs behind the saloon with tables you can practice on."

"We can't practice on this one?" Cue Ball asked.

"Nobody shoots on this one until we start the games tomorrow."

"Who's playin' first?" Fast Eddie asked.

"That'll be posted on the wall in the saloon in the morning," Jerry said. "I'm pulling the names out of a hat tonight."

"We only get your word for that?" Gentleman Lou asked.

"Anybody who wants to be present when the names are drawn is welcome to attend," Jerry said. "In fact, I'll do it at nine a.m. in the saloon. How's that?"

"Works for me," Lou said.

"Then I guess we're done here," Jerry said.

"How about drinks on the house?" Cue Ball asked.

"I don't own the saloon," Jerry said. "Take it up with the bartender."

As the people filed out, Jerry checked his watch.

"I'm gonna meet with the poker players next," he told Clint. "You want to come?"

"Why not?"

They left the pool room and walked down the hall to another door, which Jerry opened. Inside were six men and a large poker table. Clint did not know any of the men.

Since Clint wasn't playing in the poker game, Jerry didn't introduce him. He just laid out the rules and regulations and asked if anyone had any questions.

"Yeah," one man asked, "is your bodyguard there gonna be in the room while we play?"

"Mr. Adams is not my bodyguard," Jerry said. "He's my guest, and he's playing in the pool match."

"Adams?" the man said. "Would that be Clint Adams, the Gunsmith?"

"That's right," Jerry said.

"Hell, I heard you was a poker player, not a pool player," the man said.

"I'm trying to branch out."

"Well, that's fine with me," another man said. "I don't relish going up against a man who's played with the likes of Bat Masterson and Ben Thompson."

Another man said, "Oh, I don't know. I'd like to play against some big names. Might learn somethin'."

"You could afford to learn a thing or two, Henry," still another man said.

"Yeah," Henry said, "we'll see who learns something, Matt."

"The game is to begin in the morning, at ten a.m.,"

Jerry said. "Get a good night's sleep and a good break-fast. If you're not here when we start, you won't be al-lowed in."

As the men filed out of the room, the one called Henry stopped in front of Clint. He stuck his hand out.

"Just wanted to introduce myself, Mr. Adams. My name's Henry Grayson."

"Good to meet you," Clint said, shaking the man's hand.

"Good luck in your pool tournament," Grayson said. "I hope we both win."

"Thanks," Clint said, "good luck to you, too."

Grayson left.

"Any good?" Clint asked.

"Supposed to be," Jerry said. "Haven't seen him play, myself."

Clint and Jerry went down to the bar for a beer. Clint could hear the clicking of balls from the back room as the players practiced.

"Maybe I should get some practice in, too," Clint said.

"No," Jerry said. "Don't."

"Why not?"

"I don't want anybody seeing you play before the games start. I don't want your odds going down."

"But am I good enough to win the whole thing?" Clint said.

"You're already the best natural player I've ever seen, Clint," Jerry said. "You are going to bet that five hun-dred on yourself, right?"

"Oh, yeah," Clint said. "Who the hell else would I bet it on?"

TEN

The desk clerk called Clint over as he walked across the lobby.

"A message for you, sir," the clerk said, handing him a folded slip of paper.

"Thank you."

He walked away from the desk and unfolded the note. It was from Lady Eight Ball—Antonia Delaware:

Please meet me for dinner in the hotel dining room at 6 o'clock.

Whatever she wanted, she didn't care if anyone saw them together. He folded the note and put it in his pocket, then went up to his room to change for dinner.

When he entered the dining room, Lady Eight Ball wasn't there yet. When he was seated, he picked out his own table, one in a corner from where he could see the doorway. When she arrived, she stopped right in the doorway, attracting the attention of everyone in the room.

When Clint stood up and waved, she smiled and

walked over. She was wearing a gown with a low-cut front, showing an impressive amount of firm, smooth cleavage. She had worked a long time on her hair, which gleamed.

"I'm so glad you accepted my invitation," she said. As he held her chair for her, he breathed in her scent. He was immediately hard. He was excited, and had been in that state since Julia had "tested" him.

"Thank you for inviting me," he said, sitting across from her.

"And since I invited you, dinner will be on me," she said. "I insist."

"That's fine," Clint said. "I have no problem with a lady buying me dinner."

"Good," she said. "Then we're getting off on the right . . . foot."

The waiter came over and Antonia ordered a bottle of champagne.

"What are we celebrating?" he asked. "Or do you drink champagne all the time?"

"Not all the time," she said, "but quite often. However, in this instance let's call it a celebration."

"Then my question stands," he said. "What are we celebrating?"

"Well," she said, "for one thing, in a couple of hours—maybe less—we'll be upstairs in one of our rooms fucking our brains out."

He stared at her.

"Sorry, is my language too harsh? Or am I too aggressive?"

"Negative on both parts," he said. "But you wanted to shock me, didn't you?"

She smiled.

"Yes, I did," she said, "but I meant what I said. Didn't you feel it right from the start? On the platform? I mean, out of all these men . . ."

"Yes, okay," he said. "I knew it."

"See, I knew you did."

The waiter came with the champagne on ice in a metal bucket.

"Shall I pour, madam?" he asked.

"Please do."

The waiter poured out two glasses and then asked, "Are you ready to order?"

"You look like a steak man," she said.

Clint nodded, but that wasn't impressive. Most men in the West ate steak.

"Two steak dinners, please," she said, "with everything."

"Yes, madam."

He left and she sipped her champagne, regarding Clint over the rim of her glass.

"And . . . ?" he asked.

"And what?"

"There's an 'and,'" he said, "or a 'but.' One of them."

She smiled. It lit up the room, and made his groin ache.

"You're good," she said. "I've heard your reputation, but I wanted to see for myself."

"See what?"

"If you're as smart as you are famous."

"Let's concede that I'm smart," he said. "What's next? The offer?"

"I thought I made my offer."

"That wasn't an offer," he said. "That was a foregone conclusion."

This time a laugh came with the smile.

"All right, then," she said. "The offer."

ELEVEN

"There are only two players in this tournament I fear," Antonia told him over their steaks. "Fast Eddie . . . and you."

"Me? Why me?"

"Because I don't know anything about you," she said. "I mean, as far as pool goes. I've never seen you shoot, I've never heard anything about you playing pool. You're a total unknown, which is reason enough to be afraid of you."

"I suppose that makes sense."

"So I'm proposing a partnership."

"What kind of partnership?"

"You and me, whoever wins, we split the prize money."

"What's the split?"

"Sixty-forty."

"In whose favor?"

"Mine."

"Why yours?"

"Because I'm more likely to win," she said. "I have the experience."

Clint shook his head.

"What?" she asked.

"I never take less than fifty percent in any partnership," he said.

"Is that a hard-and-fast rule?"

"It is."

She cut a piece of meat, popped it into her mouth, and chewed thoughtfully.

"All right," she said, after swallowing. "It's a deal."

"No."

"What do you mean, no?"

"I don't accept your deal."

"Why not?"

"Because I'm going to be betting on myself," he said, "and I expect to win. I'd suggest you hedge your bet by wagering on me. That way if you win, you win, and if I win, you win."

She sat back and looked at him.

"You're either very confident, or very foolish."

"I guess," he said, "that'll be for you to find out."

"You mean, the hard way," she said.

He nodded.

"By playing."

Over dessert she asked, "How did you get roped into this?"

"Roped?"

"If you played pool seriously, a man with your reputation, I would have heard about it. Was it Sacks? He's paying you to play for him?"

"Jerry's my friend."

She waited for more, and when none was forthcoming, she asked, "That's it? That's your explanation?"

"That's the only explanation I've got for you."

She stared at him and shook her head.

"You're not very helpful," she said.

"Sorry."

"But I'll give you a chance to be more cooperative."

"You will? How?"

"Well," she said, "you may not want to partner with me on the pool table, but I still want to have sex."

TWELVE

Clint and Antonia walked across the hotel lobby together.

"How did you get the name 'Lady Eight Ball'?" he asked.

She laughed.

"I gave that name to myself."

"Why?" he asked. "The name you have is so . . ."

"Pretty?"

"Colorful."

"Well, I picked the name out myself."

"Why?"

"Men like nicknames," she said. "They respect them. Look at you, for instance?"

"Point taken."

They went up the stairs to the second floor.

"My room or yours?" she asked.

"I have a suite."

"Your room it is."

They walked to his door and he unlocked it and let her precede him into the room.

"Very nice," she said as he closed the door behind them. "Looks like a smaller version of San Francisco."

"That's what I thought," he said. "Drink? I have some brandy here, compliments of the hotel."

"That sounds good," she said. She walked to the doorway and peered in at the bed.

"In a hurry?" he asked.

She turned as he approached her, carrying two glasses. She accepted the glass, then stepped up to him and kissed him on the mouth.

"Neither of us seems to be in a desperate hurry," she said. "Sometimes slow is better, don't you think?"

"Sometimes," he said, and kissed her this time.

"Mmm," she said as the kiss went on a little longer. "Okay, maybe now I'm starting to be in a little more of a hurry."

She sipped the brandy again, then set it down, put her arms around his neck, and pulled him down into a deep, passionate kiss that went on for a very long time.

She pressed her pelvis against his and said, "I think somebody else is in more of a hurry, too."

They kissed again.

In the bar Fast Eddie, Gentleman Lou, and a man named Steve "Chalk" Franklin were having a drink after a few hours of practice.

"Whataya think of Clint Adams playin'?" Franklin asked.

"Interesting," Fast Eddie said.

"He's a gunman," Gentleman Lou said. "How much of a danger can he be?"

"Unless he shoots one of us," Franklin said.

"You guys are forgettin' somethin'," Fast Eddie told them.

"Like what?" Franklin asked.

"Sacks obviously picked Adams to replace him when he hurt his back—if he hurt his back. Why would he pick him if he couldn't play?"

Lou and Franklin looked at each other.

"He's got a point," Lou said. "There's a lot of money at stake."

"Yeah, but," Franklin said, "he ain't even down here practicin'."

"Maybe," Fast Eddie said, "he's just that good."

"You think so?" Franklin asked.

"Either that or he doesn't want the odds going down on Adams," the Gentleman said.

"It's a good gamble," Eddie said.

"Sonofabitch. The Gunsmith?" Franklin said. "A pool ringer?"

"You want to make that accusation to his face?" Eddie asked.

"Not me," Franklin said.

"And not me either," Eddie said. "So there's only one thing for us to do."

"What's that?" Franklin asked.

"Play our best," Eddie said, "and beat him."

Franklin picked up his beer.

"I'll drink to that," Franklin said.

"Me, too," Gentleman Lou said.

They all raised their glasses and drank to playing and winning.

THIRTEEN

They drank several more glasses of brandy in between kisses. At one point, an article of clothing began to come off with each drink, with each kiss.

Finally, it came time for Antonia to remove the article of clothing Clint was most waiting to fall, and her full breasts came into view. He caught his breath. They were perfectly shaped, like ripe melons, with dark, turgid nipples.

"My God," he said, "you're beautiful."

"And you're next," she said.

She looked down at the piece of cloth that held his bulge. She reached out and stroked him through the cotton of his underwear. Her nails sent shivers through him.

He drank the last of the brandy in his glass, staring at her breasts, the bulge of his penis swelling even larger. Finally, he set the glass down and stepped out of his underwear. His penis sprang out at her, solid, slightly curved.

"Oh, my," she said.

He was completely naked now, but there was still a

wisp of silk between then. Through it he could see the darkness of her pubic thatch. She still had some brandy in her glass, so she finished it, and set her glass down. She slid her thumbs into the waist of her panties and then slid them down to the floor. The light from the lamp made her copper pubic patch seem to glow.

"And now here we are," he said, his penis throbbing.

She came close to him, reached out, and took him in her hand, stroking him. He caught his breath, then caught it again as her hand closed tightly around him.

"Come with me," she said, tugging him by his cock, "I think we've waited long enough."

She pulled him along with her to the bedroom, used her other hand to pull the bedclothes down while holding on to him. Then she slid onto the bed and pulled him onto it with her.

"Lie back," she said. "I want to see how you smell, and taste and feel."

"My pleasure," he said.

She crawled on top of him and began to keep her word. She kissed his mouth, then his neck, his chest, his belly, and farther down. She briefly brushed his penis with her mouth, then continued down. She rubbed her face against his inner thighs, then licked and kissed them. Moving up again, this time she licked his balls, then took them in her mouth one at a time, sucking on them.

Clint moaned and reached down to cup the back of her head. She licked his balls some more, tickling them with the tip of her tongue, then moved her attention to his shaft. She licked him up and down, wetting him, then worked her way to the top and popped the bulbous head of his cock into her mouth. Slowly, she slid her mouth down, taking the length of him inside. He lifted his hips as she suckled him, and then her head began to bob up and down as she rode him with her mouth.

She moaned while she worked on him, ran her hands over his thighs, then up over his stomach and chest. Abruptly, while her hands were on his chest, he grabbed her wrists and pulled her up until she was lying prone on him.

He kissed her, then held her tightly and rolled over, reversing their positions.

"My turn to do the tasting . . ."

Jerry Sacks had lied when he said he didn't own the Alhambra Hotel and Saloon. It was all his. He was sitting in his office in back of the hotel when the door opened and his wife, Julia, walked in.

"Come to watch?" he asked. "We don't start 'til morning."

"No," she said, "I came to talk to you about your friend."

"Clint? What about him?"

"Earlier this week, when you left us alone?" she said. "He tried to rape me."

"Rape you?"

"Well, okay, he didn't try to rape me," she said, "but he tried to get me to sleep with him."

He stared at her.

"Well, aren't you going to say something?" she demanded. "Or do something?"

"Why would you even say such a thing, Julia?" he asked.

"What do you mean?"

"I mean you're lying."

"Why would I lie?"

"That's what I just asked you," he said. "It sounds more likely to me that you tried to get Clint to have sex with you, and he turned you down. What I can't figure out is why you're telling me this now, when you didn't mention it over the last few days."

"I don't believe—"

"I mean, you must have been mad all this time. Did you just decide to take your revenge now? Tonight?"

"And you wonder why we have trouble in our marriage," she said.

"I know why we have trouble," he said. "I was foolish enough to marry a young woman who obviously was only interested in my money."

"Well, if that's what you think—"

"That's what I know, Julia," he said. "Now, if you'll excuse me, I have some work to do."

"So you're not even going to entertain the possibility that I might be telling the truth?"

He put his pen down and stared at her.

"Clint Adams is my friend," he said. "What you're suggesting is just something he would never do. Now go home, Julia. Or go wherever it is you want to go. Just leave me alone."

FOURTEEN

Julia left her husband's office with a very satisfied grin on her face. From the Alhambra, she walked to a part of town a lady shouldn't be seen in. She wasn't afraid of being spotted for just that reason. There were no other town ladies in that area.

She went to a run-down hotel, entered, and stopped at the front desk long enough to make her weekly payment to the clerk, who accepted the money without looking at her face.

From there she went down the first-floor hall to a room all the way at the end and entered without knocking.

"It's about time," said the man on the bed. "I been waitin' an hour."

"Good things come to those who wait," she said. "Didn't you know that, Frank?"

"Well, then, get your good thing into this bed, Mrs. Sacks," Frank Burkett said. "I got a good thing right here waitin' for ya." He grabbed his crotch through his pants.

Julia took off her clothes, while Frank slid his pants

off and tossed them aside. She liked Burkett because, if it wasn't for him, she would have gone crazy a long time ago. Meeting him at this hotel several times a week at least kept her partially satisfied.

She watched as he stroked his abnormally large penis. She'd never known a man who liked to touch himself as much as he did. By the time she got to the bed, his cock was a raging monster.

However large it may have been, though, it was an ugly thing, with thick veins and an odd twist. Also, he didn't know how to use it. All he liked to do was stick it in, rut around for as long as it took for him to spurt, and he was done.

Julia had to slow him down, show him how to let her have some fun for a while before he stuffed it in her and had his way. That was why she was only partially satisfied. She had a man at home who couldn't satisfy her—literally—and one here who didn't know how.

She joined him on the bed and settled down between his outstretched legs. She licked and stroked him while he moaned and jerked, enjoyed the hard feel of him in her hand and her mouth. God, if he only knew how to use this thing, she thought, these meetings would be Heaven, rather than haven.

She enjoyed his cock as long as he would let her, but then he flipped her over violently and rammed himself home. While he pounded away at her, she took hold of the bedpost above her and thought about Clint Adams. If all the stories about him and his women were true, he could have been the answer to her prayers but he had rejected her. She never really expected Jerry to believe her story about Clint trying to take her to bed, but she had thought of another way to make not only Clint Adams pay, but her husband as well.

She just had to wait for Burkett to be finished so she could tell him her plan.

"You want me to do what?" Burkett asked.

"Rob my husband's game," she said, "and kill him."

He laughed.

"Is that all?"

"You're not afraid to rob him, are you, Frank?" she asked, stroking his penis at the same time. It was larger soft than a hard cock she'd seen on another man. But, good God, it was not a pretty sight. At least when it was in her mouth, or her pussy, she didn't have to look at it.

"I ain't afraid of nothin'," he told her.

"Well, the . . ."

"Give me one good reason why I should kill your husband?" he asked.

She ran her fingernail along the underside of his dick, causing it to twitch.

"If he dies," she said, "I inherit everything he owns, and you get to keep all the money you get from the robbery."

He took one of her full breasts in his huge hand and squeezed until a tear fell from her eye.

"Plus I get you, right?"

"Of course, darling," she said, stroking him, "you'll always have me."

And just like that the monster was awake again. He tried to roll her over but she stopped him.

"What do you say?"

"I say lemme think about it," he said. "I'll have to

come up with some good boys to do the job with me. But I'll think about it later."

She allowed him to push her onto her back and then straddle her. At least she'd succeeded in getting him to think about it.

FIFTEEN

They lay with their legs intertwined, despite the sheen of sweat that covered them both.

"I need a bath," Antonia said.

"Me, too."

"Can we get one this late?"

Clint looked at her.

"Well, we're players, right?" he asked. "All our needs are supposed to be met."

"Really?" She pushed herself up onto one elbow. "A late-night bath?"

"I'll go down and arrange it."

He got out of bed and pulled on his pants.

They sat in the bathtub together, her back against his chest, and soaked.

"This is so decadent," she said.

He slid his hands from her shoulders down to her breasts and cupped them, flicking the nipples with his thumbs.

"You're a decadent woman, aren't you?" he asked.

"I'm a small-town woman who got out as soon as she could," she said. "You know what my real name is?"

"You mean it isn't Antonia Delaware?"

"No."

"And it isn't Lady Eight Ball."

She laughed and said, "No."

"So why would you want me to know your real name?" he asked.

"I don't know," she said. "I just do."

He started to slide his hands off her breasts but she pressed hers over his, holding them there.

"Wanda."

"What?"

"I know," she said. "Wanda Mae Smith."

"Oh."

"When I was fifteen, I left home and changed my name to Antonia," she said. "When I was twenty, I picked up a pool cue, and it felt good in my hands. From that day on, I've been playing."

"And how old are you now?" he asked.

She elbowed him and said, "Now that I'm not going to tell you."

"So you made yourself into a pool player," he said, "and a lady."

"I made myself a pool player," she said, "but a woman named Laurie Davenport made me a lady. Took me under her wing, showed me how to dress, and walk, and talk, and eat properly."

"Where is she now?"

"She died a few years ago," she said. "I've been on my own since then."

She wiggled up more tightly against him. His penis began to crawl up the crack in her ass, and her lower back.

"There's something very important you have to know, Clint."

"What's that?"

"I was never a whore."

"I didn't think you were."

"Men tend to think that when a woman makes her own way, she makes it on her back," she said. "I made my way on a pool table."

"It couldn't have been easy," he said.

"It wasn't," she said. "It took a long time to get men to take me seriously."

"But now they do," he said.

"Some of them do," she said. "Some men will never accept that a woman can make her own way without a man, and on her own two feet."

"Then you should be very proud of yourself."

"I am," she said. "I'm very proud."

He removed his hands from her breasts and soaped her back for her.

"We should go upstairs," she said, leaning her head against his chest.

"In a minute," he said.

After a few minutes she said, "Have you given my offer any more thought?"

"No," he said. "We've been busy."

"Well, then," she said, "forget I said anything, okay?"

"Sure," he said, "okay."

"I'll just beat everybody myself, and make off with the money," she said.

"Good for you," he said. "Good."

SIXTEEN

Burkett watched while Julia got dressed.

"Are you thinking?" she asked.

"Yes, I am."

She noticed where he was looking.

"I mean, thinking about the proposal I made," she said.

"About robbing your husband, and killing him?"

"Yes."

"Remind me of what I get."

"All the money from the game," she said. "The pool game, and the poker game."

"And?"

"And me."

"And with you, everything that Mr. Sacks has now, right?"

"That's right."

"I'll have to pay some men to help me," he said.

"How many?"

He thought a moment while she buttoned her dress.

"Four."

"How much will you have to pay them?"

"Well . . . I don't wanna have to pay them. Not out of my end anyway."

"You want me to pay them?" she asked.

"That would be good."

She set her jaw.

"How much?"

"That depends."

"On what?"

"If we don't tell them how much we're gettin'," he said, "we can probably get them for about a hundred dollars each."

"And if we tell them?"

"They'll want a cut."

"But if you get four men who will take a hundred dollars," she said, "they won't be very smart, or very good."

"That's true," he said, "but how smart do you they have to be to do what I tell them to do? And how good do they have to be to rob a bunch of gamblers?"

"You forgot one thing," she said.

"What?"

"Clint Adams is playing pool."

"Adams?"

"He's been staying at the house, Frank."

"I know that," he said, "but I didn't know he was gonna play. That changes things. I'll need four good boys."

"All right," she said, standing up after pulling on her boots. "You get four good boys, and I'll pay them."

"Okay."

"I have to go."

He was lying on his back, still naked. He took his penis in his hand and waved it at her.

"You sure?"

"Yes, Frank," she said. "I'm, sure."

"Well, when will I see you again? I mean, here."

"As soon as you have your four men picked out, let me know," she said. "And don't take too long. This tournament will only take a few days."

"Okay," Burkett said. "I'll get the boys together tomorrow."

"Okay," she said, "then I'll meet you here again tomorrow night and we can go over the plan."

"Don't you think I should take care of the plannin'?" he asked. "After all, I'm the man."

"Yeah, you're the man," she said, "but do you know all the entrances and exits to that building?"

"No."

"Then we'll meet here tomorrow night and go over the plan. Okay?"

"Okay, Julia," he said, waving his dick at her again. "Okay."

SEVENTEEN

After their bath they decided that Antonia would go back to her room and they'd both get some much-needed sleep.

In the morning Clint dressed and went down to the dining room for breakfast. Other players—both pool and poker—were already there, but none invited him to sit with them. Others came in after him, but they all went to other tables to either sit alone, or sit with some other players they knew.

When Antonia came down, she got everyone's attention, and all the men watched her walk directly to Clint's table.

"Do you mind if I join you?" she asked.

"Not at all," he said.

She sat and ordered what he had, a steak-and-egg breakfast.

"I like a woman with a big appetite," he said.

"I have big appetites," she said. "Plural—but then you already know that."

Clint poured her some coffee while they waited for her breakfast.

"Why are you all alone?" she asked, looking around.

"The simple answer is that nobody wanted to eat with me," he said.

"They're probably afraid of you," she said. "After all, you're the big bad gunman."

"Yes, I am."

"You're also the unknown factor," she said. "I'd expect somebody to try to get something out of you."

"Maybe they think you are," Clint said, "and you'll pass along whatever you find out."

"Why would you say that?"

"Well," he said, "you offered to partner with me. Maybe when I turned you down, you decided to partner with somebody else?"

"That would either make me shrewd," she said, "or a bitch."

"Sleeping together has got nothing to do with the match," he said, "so I'd say it would make you shrewd."

"Maybe I should have done that," she said. "Who would you suggest I partner with?"

"I don't know," he said. "I don't know these men, haven't seen them play. You have. But according to Sacks, Fast Eddie is probably the one to beat."

"Is that what he said?"

"Well," Clint replied, "he said either Eddie, or you."

The waiter came with her breakfast, and a fresh pot of coffee.

"Well, you've seen most of these men play," Clint said. "Do you agree with Sacks's assessment?"

"Me or Eddie?" she asked. "Yes, I can see that. Gentleman Lou shoots a good stick as well."

"Well, maybe one of you will draw the other today, and save me having to play that one."

"That would be good for you, or for me, if it happens," she said. "Maybe Lou and Eddie will match up."

"Whatever happens," Clint said, "I'll have to watch and learn."

"Learn the game?"

"No," he said, "I mean learn the players. I do that when I'm going to play poker at a strange table. Watch for a while, pick out the dangerous opponents."

"Sounds like that would work in pool also," she said.

From breakfast they all adjourned to the saloon. Seemed like every one of the players wanted to be present for the drawing of names. The poker players were already upstairs in their room, as no names had to be drawn. The pool players were all sitting at one large table.

"Gentlemen," Sacks said, "and lady, we will commence with the drawing of names. The first two names I draw will play first, and then so on. Here we go. The names are all in this bowl, which the bartender will draw from."

Sacks held the bowl, and the bartender stuck his hand in, pulling out a slip of paper.

"Lady Eight Ball," Sacks read, then waited for the bartender to hand him the second name, "will play Chet McDermott."

There was a smattering of applause as the two players acknowledged their match.

"Next game will match . . ." He waited. "Clint Adams with . . . Lenny Wilson, known to most of us as Cue Ball."

"Tossing you right in with the pros," Antonia said.

"That's okay," Clint said. "I'm ready, but first I'm going to watch your match."

EIGHTEEN

The game was straight pool. At 1 point per ball, the first player to get 150 points was the winner. You had to call the pocket you were going to sink your ball into.

To determine who would break first, each player had to hit a ball off the far cushion. It had to come back, strike the near cushion, and the player whose ball stopped closest to that near cushion broke first.

"Watch this," Jerry Sacks said to Clint. "She's death on this."

Sure enough, Antonia's ball stopped closest to the cushion. She broke, sank a ball immediately on the break, then went on to sink 41 more balls before missing. She had the lead, 42–0, before her opponent even got to the table.

McDermott stepped up to the table, sank 20 balls in a row before missing what looked like an easy shot.

Antonia stepped up to the table, sank 26 more balls before missing. One hour in and she now led 68–20.

"She's stringin' him along," Jerry said.

He and Clint were watching, as were several of the

other players. For the most part, the players who weren't involved were not there. They were probably downstairs practicing, or playing some side games for money against each other. Jerry had warned Clint not to get into any side games. He didn't want anyone seeing Clint shoot until his first match.

"You mean she missed on purpose?"

Jerry nodded.

"She wants to make him overeager."

McDermott started shooting, but after he sank the eighth ball in a row, he missed. He cursed himself and stalked away from the table. Lady Eight Ball now led 68–28.

"She's got him nervous," Jerry said.

"But why wouldn't she just sink as many balls as she can?" Clint asked.

"She will now," Jerry said. "He's nervous, and he's mad at himself. She'll try to put him away now, but if he gets to the table again, he'll be a mess mentally. Watch."

Jerry turned out to be a prophet.

It looked as if Antonia was going to "run the table."

She made amazing shots—bank shots, combinations, everything you could think of. On the seventy-eighth ball of the run, she caught a bad roll and missed. She now had a lead of 145–28. McDermott was destroyed. He sank 8 balls, then missed.

Antonia quickly stepped up to the table and sank 5 balls.

"Lady Eight Ball wins," Jerry announced.

McDermott, dripping with sweat after two hours, shook her hand quickly and stalked from the room—angry and embarrassed.

"Congratulations," Clint said. "You played—both the player and the game."

"Thank you," she said. "McDermott plays well when he breaks out on top. When he's behind, he gets nervous and anxious."

"You certainly knew your opponent," he said.

"It's a very important part of the game," she said. "I'm going to go freshen up, and then come and watch you play. That is, unless the game ends quickly."

As she left, he wondered if she was trying to play with his head. The one area of the game he was certainly lacking in was knowing his opponents. He only had what Jerry Sacks told him.

NINETEEN

Clint stepped to the table, shook hands with Cue Ball Wilson, and then they shot for the break. Cue Ball easily beat him, as Clint hit his ball too hard. But this was not the part of the game Jerry told Clint he was a natural for.

"Your eye for seeing shots, lining them up, and your uncanny ability to make combinations. It's everything that makes you a dead show with a gun."

Cue Ball broke, sank a ball on the break, and then calmly and coolly sank 88 balls in a row. Clint was beginning to wonder if he'd ever get to the table. Finally he did, when his opponent missed the eighty-ninth ball.

With the score 88–0, Clint stepped up to the table and immediately made a combination shot that had the spectators leaning forward. From there, he sank 136 balls in a row, feeling more and more comfortable as he went along. If anything, he missed because he got overconfident. He vowed never to do that again—if he got to the table a second time. Cue Ball Wilson was very good. Certainly a good enough player to overcome a 136–88 deficit.

But Cue Ball seemed a bit rattled by Clint's run. Having someone come out of nowhere and make a run like that started him thinking that if *he* missed, *he* might never get back to the table.

Off to one corner, Jerry Sacks was looking extremely satisfied with himself.

Cue Ball began to shoot, and after 11 balls he missed an easy shot. Looking annoyed and puzzled, Cue Ball withdrew from the table.

Clint stepped up and sank the remaining 14 balls. This match was over in an hour.

"Clint Adams wins," Sacks said.

Clint stepped up to Sacks and accepted a handshake. At that point Antonia entered the room and took everything in. The room took her in, too. She was wearing a dress that hugged her, and she smelled as if she was fresh from a bath.

"Over already?" she asked.

"Afraid so," Clint said, "although it seemed almost . . . too easy."

"What do you mean?"

"For a talented pool player, Cue Ball Wilson went away surprisingly quick," Clint said.

"How many balls did you sink in a row?" she asked.

"A hundred and thirty-six."

She stared at him.

"In a row?"

"Yes."

"Then Cue Ball didn't go away easily," she said. "You put him away."

"Next competitors," Jerry called.

"Do you want to watch?" she asked Clint.

"No," he said. "I think I'll go and watch the poker game for a while."

"Then I'm going to do some shopping," she said. "Dinner together later?"

"Sure," he said. "Let's meet in the lobby."

"Why in the lobby?" she asked. "Why don't we meet in your suite?"

"Because if we meet there," he said, "we might not get to dinner."

"And that would be a bad thing?" she asked.

"Only because I think I'm going to need all my strength for later," he said.

She smiled and said, "Well, that I can guarantee."

TWENTY

Clint spent a couple of hours watching the poker game.

And realized how easily he could be making money there. There wasn't a really good poker player among them. He finally gave up watching, then headed back to his suite. He had to pass the room where the pool matches were taking place and saw Jerry Sacks standing out in the hall.

"Getting bored?" Clint asked.

Sacks looked at him and said, "Fast Eddie's giving his opponent a pool lesson in there. It'll be over soon. I wanted to see if I could catch you out here."

"What for?"

"To tell you how great you were," Sacks said excitedly. "I've already made a bundle betting on you against Cue Ball."

"Maybe I should have gotten down on that, too," Clint said.

"Don't worry," Jerry said, "I made a bet for you."

"You did? Well, thanks. Where's the money?"

"I've got it, but I'm thinking we should let it ride. Whataya say?"

"Who am I playing next?"

"Well, Antonia will play the winner of this match, and you'll play the winner of the next one," Jerry said.

"Who's playing the next one?"

"Gentleman Lou is playing a guy named Roker, who I've never heard of, but who I also hear is not that good."

"So it looks like I'll be shooting against Gentleman Lou next?"

Sacks nodded.

"Even with the way you shot against Cue Ball, we should get ten to one or better on you against him. Everyone will expect him to roll right over you."

"And he won't?"

"Damn right, he won't," Sacks said. "You're going to shock him and everyone else."

"Okay, then," Clint said. "Let the money ride."

He had bet his five hundred on himself to win the whole shebang. He hadn't thought about betting each individual match.

"Wait a minute," he said. "So Antonia will be playing Fast Eddie next?"

"Yep," he said.

"When?"

"That'll be tomorrow," Jerry said. "We still got a few matches to get to today."

"You going to bet that game?"

"I am."

"Who are you taking?"

"Eddie."

"Can Antonia beat him?"

"Maybe, but I don't think so."

"What kind of odds would I get betting on her?"

"Against Eddie? Four, maybe five to one. But you don't want to do that, Clint."

"Why not?"

"If you're thinking of betting on her, go inside and watch the end of this match. Watch Eddie shoot before you bet against him. That's my advice."

"Okay," Clint said. "I'll take your advice. Let's go in and watch the end of the match."

Clint watched closely as Eddie shot. He was methodical and, at times, almost like a magician.

"Has his opponent shot yet?" Clint asked Jerry, keeping his voice low.

"Hasn't got to the table yet," Jerry said. "Eddie sank two balls on the break, and has been sinking them ever since."

"So he might win without letting his opponent even shoot?"

"That's the way he likes to win."

When Clint and Eddie reentered the room, Eddie was ahead 121–0. Clint stood and watched while Eddie went ahead and sank 29 more balls without even a near miss.

"Game!" Jerry called. "One hundred and fifty to nothing."

Eddie's opponent shook his head, shook hands with Eddie, and left in a daze.

"That was incredible," Clint said to Eddie, shaking his hand.

"I heard you weren't so bad yourself," Eddie said. He looked at Jerry. "Who's my next opponent?"

"Lady Eight Ball."

"She shoot well this morning?" he asked.

"Very well," Jerry said.

"She's good," Eddie said. "It'll be a challenge."

Eddie left the room, taking his stick with him. It was his own.

"Still want to bet against him?" Jerry asked.

"I don't think so," Clint said.

"Smart move."

"But I won't bet on him either."

"You and Antonia that close already, are you?" Jerry asked.

"We're friends," Clint said.

"Well, if she managed to beat Eddie, and you beat Lou, how friendly will the two of you be if you have to face each other?"

"Competition is one thing," Clint said, "friendship is another. I can keep them apart."

Jerry shook his head.

"What?" Clint asked.

"Maybe you can keep them separate," Jerry said, "but I don't think she can."

TWENTY-ONE

Frank Burkett nursed a beer at the Alhambra Saloon, listening to the conversations going on around him. Eventually, a couple of pool players made their way to the bar—losers, apparently—and talked about all the money they had lost.

"I can't believe the way that Adams shot," one man said. "I think Sacks brought in a ringer. Nobody can shoot like that who ain't played the game his whole life."

"You think that's bad, I got beat by that bitch, Lady Eight Ball." The man snorted. "What a name!"

"I got a good mind to get a gun and just take the prize money," the first man said.

"What would you do with a gun?" the other man asked, laughing. "You'd shoot your foot off."

"It wouldn't be so hard," the first man said. "Did you notice there ain't no security?"

"What kind of security do ya need?" the second man asked. "You got the Gunsmith, and at least half of the other players are armed."

"There's a way," the first man said.

"Like how?"

"Like usin' your brain," the first man said.

"Well," the other man admitted, "that'd be better than charging in there with guns out, trying to rob the place."

"I gotta go pack," the first man said. "I gotta get out of town before I decide to go ahead and give it a try."

"Yeah, me, too," the second man said.

They finished their beers and left the saloon.

That was the conversation Burkett had been waiting to hear. It gave him some of the information he needed, especially about security. Julia couldn't answer those questions for him.

He ordered a second beer, decided to go to a table and think things over for a while. He already knew what four men he'd use to rob the game, but now he was having second thoughts. It was like the two men had said—if he used his brain, he could figure something out.

And it didn't take long. An idea occurred to him, and the more he thought about it, the better it sounded. He just had to be careful not to tell Julia what he was going to do. She'd start bitching at him, and she was good at that. He usually stopped her bitching by sticking his dick in her—she loved that—but if he had to, he'd just give her a slap to shut her up. Probably what her husband should have done since the first day of their marriage. Then maybe she wouldn't be spending her afternoons in a run-down hotel jumping up and down on Burkett's dick.

Burkett wasn't the only one who overheard the conversation of the two pool players, though. Two men at the other end of the bar had listened intently when they heard the reference to "that kind of money."

Wilson Tulley nudged his partner, Austin Davis, and said, "You hear that?"

"I heard it," Davis said.

"Whataya think?"

"I think there's a lot of money up on the second floor," Davis said. "All we gotta do is figure out a way to get our hands on it."

"Won't be easy," Tulley said. "Not with the Gunsmith up there."

"He's shootin' pool," Davis said. "That takes both hands."

"You're right," Davis said. "If we can catch him bent over, we'd have the drop on him."

Tulley and Davis were not from Tucson. They were just passing through, stopping for a beer. They were in between bank jobs, and were looking for something quicker and easier than a bank, or a train. They were wondering if the Tucson stage carried any money when they heard the talk about the pool game.

"How much money you think they were talkin' about?" Tulley asked.

"I dunno," Davis said, "but it sounded like a lot."

"So whatta we do?"

"We keep listenin'," Davis said. "We need a little more information, like how many players there are, and what other ways there are in and out of this place."

"Well," Tulley said, "I reckon that kind of thinkin' calls for another beer."

Davis grinned and said to his friend, "I think you're right."

TWENTY-TWO

Clint had not been to see the sheriff since his arrival in town. He decided to remedy that fact with a short courtesy visit that afternoon.

He was crossing the street, approaching the sheriff's office, when the door opened and a man wearing a badge stepped out. From where Clint was, he couldn't tell if it was a deputy's badge, or if this was the sheriff.

The man stepped into the street and started crossing toward Clint, so that they literally met in the center of the street.

"Excuse me," Clint said. "Sheriff?"

"That's right," the man said, stopping. "Can I help ya?"

"Well, actually I just wanted to introduce myself. I'm—"

"Hold that thought," the lawman said, putting his hand on Clint's arm. "Let's not do this in the middle of the street, huh?"

"Agreed."

They turned and went back to where Clint had come

from, rather than the side of the street the sheriff had come from.

"Okay," the lawman said when they were on the boardwalk, "you said you wanted to introduce yourself?"

"Clint Adams," Clint said. "Got to town yesterday."

"Oh, yeah," the sheriff said. "You been a houseguest of Jerry Sacks for a while."

"That's right," Clint said. "I did sneak into town for a drink or two over the past few weeks, but now I'm staying at the Alhambra."

"You playin' in the poker tournament?"

"Pool."

"Pool." The man looked surprised. "Heard you was a poker player, but never heard anythin' about pool. Well, my name's Lambert, Tom Lambert. Welcome to Tucson."

The two men shook hands. Lambert was in his late forties, had an air of confidence about him.

"What, no warning?"

"You usually get that? Yeah, I guess you would. See, I figure I can warn you to stay out of trouble, but then some idiot with a gun and half a brain is gonna want to try you, and what are you supposed to do?"

"That's . . . an unusual attitude for a lawman to have," Clint said.

"I been a lawman a long time, Adams," Lambert said. "And you're a guest of a prominent member of the community. So I'll just say . . . do the best you can not to kill anybody, unless you have to."

"I'll do my best," Clint promised.

"Where you headed?" Lambert asked.

"Back to the saloon."

"I'll walk with you."

"Fine."

As they walked, the sheriff asked, "How are you doin' in the tournament?"

"I won my first match."

"Think you can win the whole thing?"

"I don't know," Clint said. "There are some good players, and I'm kind of new to this game. At least, at this level."

"I know what you mean," Lambert said. "I've played myself, but only to pass the time."

When they reached the saloon, Lambert said, "I'm gonna keep walkin'. Doin' my rounds."

"Come in later and I'll buy you a drink," Clint invited.

"I'll do that, thanks."

The sheriff kept walking and Clint entered the saloon.

"That's him," Davis said.

"How do you know?" Tulley asked.

"I seen him once," Davis said. "Long time ago, but he ain't changed."

"You sure?"

"Let's wait and see," Davis said, "but yeah, I'm sure."

They watched as Clint walked to the bar and ordered a beer.

"What if we take him now?" Tulley asked. "Be easier to rob the game if he wasn't around."

"Are you kiddin'?" Davis asked. "You know what kind of heat that would bring on this town? Naw, naw, we got to figure this out, Wilson. We got to be smart about this."

"Well," Tulley said, "bein' smart was always your job, Austin."

TWENTY-THREE

Clint was content.

He'd played a good game of pool, wasn't missing anything by not being in the poker game, had a satisfying meeting with the local law, was enjoying his beer, was going to have dinner with a beautiful woman, and then . . .

But that was tonight.

Tomorrow might end with him having to play Antonia, and according to Jerry Sacks, they wouldn't be able to maintain their "friendship" after that.

Clint had a hard time believing that two adults could not separate business from pleasure. He was going to have to talk to her about that at dinner. Or maybe a little later . . .

Of course, she had to beat Fast Eddie first. Maybe he'd wait and see if that happened before he brought the subject up.

"You look like you lost your best friend," somebody said.

Clint turned and found himself looking into the face of Gentleman Lou Teacher.

"Hello, Lou. Buy you a drink?"

"Don't see why not," Gentleman Lou said. "I'll have a beer."

Clint ordered two fresh beers and handed one to Lou.

"Looks like you and me tomorrow," Gentleman Lou said.

"Should be interesting," Clint said.

"I heard you shot well this morning."

"I did okay."

"You'll have to do better than okay to beat me," Lou said.

"I'll try not to disappoint you."

"The only thing that would disappoint me would be if I don't win," Lou said.

"Well, if that's the case," Clint said, "I'll see what I can do to definitely disappoint you."

"I wish you luck."

They lifted their mugs to each other.

"Thanks for the drink," Lou said.

"Leaving already?"

"I've got to get my rest," Lou said. "I'm going to have some dinner, and then go to my room. I'd do the same if I was you."

"I will," Clint said, "in a while."

Gentleman Lou took a step back and studied Clint for a few moments.

"You ain't a bit worried, are you?"

"Lou," Clint said, "I've faced hundreds of men with guns who wanted to kill me. Facing you across a pool table doesn't worry me."

"Well," Lou said, "I guess when you put it that way . . ."

He turned and walked away, not happy with the answer he'd gotten.

Clint watched him go with a small smile on his face. The smile was still there when Jerry Sacks came up alongside him.

"What are you smiling at?" Jerry asked, leaning on the bar.

"Gentleman Lou just tried to intimidate me," Clint said.

"And did he?"

Clint looked at Jerry.

"Men without guns don't intimidate me, Jerry."

"That's good," Jerry said. "You're going to have to be very good to beat him tomorrow. Better than you were today."

"I've got to tell you, I've got a bad taste in my mouth about today, Jerry."

"What do you mean?"

"Cue Ball went away too easily."

"You scared him with that run you had."

"No," Clint said, "no way."

Jerry turned his body to face Clint.

"What are you saying?"

"I'm saying he threw the match," Clint said, "and he didn't do a very good acting job while he was doing it."

Jerry stared at Clint, then called the bartender over and ordered a whiskey. When it was poured, he picked it up and downed it quickly.

"All right," he said, "okay, don't get sore."

"You paid him off."

"Yes."

"Why?"

"I thought you might need a little confidence booster,"

Jerry said, but then rushed to add, "but you didn't. By God, man, you shot a great game!"

"Jerry—"

"I swear," Jerry said, raising his hands, "no more shenanigans. It's on the up-and-up from here on in."

"It better be, Jerry," Clint said. "I don't know what else you might have had planned, but it better end here."

"It does, I swear," Jerry said. "Believe me, you don't need my help."

"Okay."

"But you do need to concentrate a little more," Jerry said, "if you're going to beat Lou."

"I concentrated today," Clint argued.

"Not on that shot you missed," Jerry said. "You could have run the whole table, Clint. One hundred and fifty balls in a row, but you lost your concentration for one split second."

Clint played with his mug for a few seconds, then put it down.

"You're right," he said. "I started to wonder how many more I could sink in a row, and I missed."

"There you go," Jerry said. "Don't ever worry about missing a shot, Clint. Just keep shooting, like a machine. Don't give yourself a chance to think."

"Okay," Clint said, "okay. I can do that."

"And I noticed you change sticks," Jerry said. "What was that about?"

"The bartender recommended it," Clint said. "He said a heavier stick might help me."

"Well," Jerry said, scratching his cheek, "I have to admit he was right. You had more control of your shots than I've ever seen."

"It'll go better tomorrow," Clint said.

"Well," Jerry said, slapping Clint on the back. "If that's true, if you shoot better tomorrow than you did today, you'll win. Lemme buy you another drink."

While they waited for a fresh beer each, Clint said, "I thought Julia was going to come and watch for a while?"

"No," Jerry said, "not today, probably not tomorrow. Why are you interested in having her watch?"

"No reason," Clint said with a shrug. "It's just that she mentioned it."

"Don't worry about my wife," Jerry said shortly. "I'll worry about her. You worry about your game."

"Okay, Jerry," Clint said as the drinks came. "You got it."

TWENTY-FOUR

Over dinner in the hotel dining room Clint told Antonia about Gentleman Lou's attempt to intimidate him.

"He was probably testing you," she said. "Wanted to see if you would rattle. You didn't, which probably bothered him."

"It did. I could see it."

"You'll do well tomorrow," she said. "You're the wild card."

"And what about you?"

"Me? Tomorrow?" she asked. "Fast Eddie? I've played against Fast Eddie before."

"And beat him?"

She shook her head.

"No," she said, "I've never beaten him before."

"Are you worried?"

"Sure I'm worried," she said, "but the odds are in my favor, aren't they? I mean, I've got to beat him sometime, right?"

He wanted to tell her that wasn't always the case.

Sometimes somebody just had your number, and the odds didn't change. They beat you every time. But he couldn't tell her that.

"Right," he said, "and I'm going to be there to watch you do it this time."

"There is one thing, though," she admitted.

"What's that?"

She reached across the table and placed her hand over his.

"If I am going to beat him, I'm going to need to be rested," she said. "That means spending the night in my own room . . . alone."

"Well, that goes for both of us, doesn't it?" he asked, taking her hand. "I'll need to be sharp to beat Gentleman Lou."

"Then you don't mind?"

"Sure I mind," he said, "but what can we do about it? We'll just wait until tomorrow night. Then we can celebrate both of us winning."

"I knew you'd understand," she said.

Neither of them mentioned that by tomorrow night they might know whether they had to play each other or not.

Wilson Tulley and Austin Davis watched Clint Adams walk into the hotel dining room. Tulley walked over and sneaked a glance, then returned.

"He's sittin' with the woman, Lady Eight Ball," he said." Did you find out who's playin' who tomorrow?"

"Ain't hard," Davis said. "All ya got to do is listen around here. Adams is playin' that Gentleman Lou guy. The woman is playin' Fast Eddie."

"Even I heard of him," Tulley said. "He's supposed to be the best."

"We could take them tomorrow, but I've got another idea," Davis said.

"What's that?"

"Let's get out of the lobby."

They went back into the saloon, got a table, then Tulley went to the bar and got two beers.

"So, what's your idea?"

Tulley drank half his beer, as if he needed it for courage, or fortitude.

"We take care of Adams first," he finally said.

"You and me, take the Gunsmith?"

"It'd probably be easier to take him alone than with a whole bunch of other pool players around. They carry guns, too."

"In the street?"

"Well," Davis said, "not in a fair fight. That's not what I'm talkin' about."

"An ambush, then?"

Davis nodded.

"We bushwhack him tomorrow, get him out of the picture," Davis said. "Then we take care of the game."

"Where do we do it?" Tulley asked.

"That's somethin' we'll have to decide," Davis said. "Let's finish our drinks and take a walk around town, find a likely place."

"How do we get him there, once we pick the place?" Tulley asked.

"That part's easy," Davis said.

"How easy?"

Davis shrugged.

"We just invite him."

TWENTY-FIVE

Burkett rolled off Julia, panting, sweating. Julia eased herself away from him, feeling chilled as the air hit her naked body, covered with his perspiration. She wanted a bath badly, but it would have to wait.

Burkett lay on his back, staring at the ceiling, catching his breath.

"Jesus," he said. "You're somethin', you know that, Julia?"

"Thank you, Frank."

"Why don't you just do this to your old man until he has a heart attack?"

"Believe me, I've thought of it," she said. "What about you?"

"Again? So soon?" he asked. "You wanna give me a heart attack?"

"That's not what I mean," she said. "I mean, did you get the men you needed?"

"Oh, them," he said. "Uh, yeah, I got 'em. They're ready to go on my say-so."

"Good," she said. "Then say so."

"When?"

"Tomorrow? Why wait?"

"Well," Burkett said, "I been listenin' to what's goin' on over there."

"What do you mean?"

"There's a poker game, too, and side bets bein' made," he said. "There's a lot of money floatin' around that place."

"There's more money in the bank, under my husband's name," she said. "And when he's dead, it's mine." She put her hand on his chest. "And I'll be yours."

"I know that, sweetie," he said, "but more money is more money. If we let the games go on just a little longer, there'll be a lot more."

She sat up, crossed her arms across her bare breasts.

"I want it done soon, Frank," she said.

"It will be done soon, Julia," Burkett said. "I promise."

The promises of men, she thought. Just another damn promise.

Clint and Antonia came out of the dining room together, into the lobby. It was after nine, and the foot traffic was down to almost nothing. And as the hotel lobby got quiet, the saloon got busier.

"Do you want a drink before you turn in?" Clint asked her.

"I don't think so," she said. "You just want to get me liquored up so you can take advantage of me."

"You might be right. How about I walk you to your room, then?"

She put her hand on his chest and said, "Same difference. I know you want to go into the saloon, so just go. I'll be fine. I can certainly find my way to my room."

"All right, Antonia," he said. "Good night."

"I'll see you in the morning," she said.

He watched her walk across the lobby until she reached the stairs. She turned and looked back at him, then started up.

He waited until she was out of sight, then walked over to the saloon entrance and went in.

TWENTY-SIX

The saloon was busy, with poker players on one side, pool players on another, and drinking and gambling townsmen in between.

Standing at the bar alone was Jerry Sacks, and he didn't look happy. Clint wondered what would happen between Sacks and his wife when this tournament was over. He walked over to join his friend.

"Dinner over?" Jerry asked.

"Antonia went to bed. She needs her rest if she's going to beat Fast Eddie."

At the mention of his name, they looked over at Fast Eddie, who was sitting with another couple of pool players who were already out of the game.

"Maybe he's giving them lessons," Clint said.

"Yeah, well, they need it," Jerry said. He called the bartender over and ordered two beers.

The bartender was Danny Troy, the man who had advised Clint to use a heavier stick.

"Your advice came in handy," Clint told him when he brought the beers.

"Yeah, I heard you won pretty easy," Troy said. "Good for you."

"When's the last time you played a serious game of pool, Mr. Troy?" Jerry asked.

"It's just Troy, Mr. Sacks. Or Danny. And I ain't played any pool for a long time. Never could figure out a way to make money at it, so I took to tendin' bar."

"What about those tables in the back room?" Jerry asked.

"I stay away from that room," Troy said. "I don't have that much willpower. 'Scuse me."

He went down the bar to serve some other customers.

"Seems to me if you'd known about him, you wouldn't have had to send for me," Clint said.

"I'm happy with what I got," Jerry said. He raised his beer mug. "Here's to tomorrow's game."

Clint lifted his mug, then they both drank.

"Jerry, you know those two men?"

"Where?" Jerry didn't turn to look.

"They're sitting two tables to Fast Eddie's right," Clint said. "They've been watching us, or me, since I walked in."

Jerry took his time, eventually gave a nonchalant look in the direction Clint was indicating.

"Don't know them," he said. "Never seen them before."

"Well, they're pretty interested in us," Clint said. "Probably me."

"Maybe they recognize you," Jerry said.

"Yeah, maybe," Clint said. "That's never good news."

"Maybe this ain't good news either," Jerry said. "Here comes the sheriff."

"Lambert," Clint said.

"You've met?"

"I stopped in to introduce myself. Invited him to have a drink."

"Well, I guess he's taking you up on it," Jerry said. "Maybe he knows those two."

"Maybe he does," Clint said. "We'll ask him."

They both turned to greet the lawman.

"Mr. Sacks, Mr. Adams," Lambert said.

"Sheriff," Jerry said.

"Come for that drink, Sheriff?" Clint asked.

"That I did."

Clint waved at Troy and ordered a beer for the sheriff.

When the sheriff had a cold beer in his hand, Clint described the table and the two men and asked Lambert if he knew them.

"Not by name," the sheriff said, "but I've seen them around town."

"How long they been in town?"

"Oh, a few days."

"Cause any trouble?"

"Nope. Why? What've they done?"

"Nothing but eyeball me since I walked in," Clint said.

"You been eyeballed before, I'll wager."

"Oh yeah," Clint said. "I was just wondering if you or Jerry could tell me anything about them."

"I guess I could find out, if you want," Lambert said. "I'll walk over there and ask them."

"Don't do that," Clint said. "At least, not now. But I'd appreciate it if you'd do it tomorrow, as if you were just doing your job. I don't want them to know I'm interested."

"Okay," Lambert said, finishing his beer. "I'll have a talk with them tomorrow and let you know what I find out."

"I'd appreciate it, Sheriff. Thanks."

"Thanks for the beer," Lambert said. "Mr. Sacks."

"Sheriff."

The lawman turned and left without a glance at the two men in question.

"He bought the sheriff a drink," Tulley said.

"I saw," Davis said.

"You think he spotted us?"

"Naw," Davis said. "If he had, he woulda sent the sheriff over to talk to us, or come over himself. Just the same, though, we better get out of here."

"Yeah, right."

They tossed down the rest of their drinks and walked across the floor to the exit. As far as they could see, Clint Adams never looked at them.

Clint followed the progress of the two men in the mirror behind the bar.

"They gone?" he asked Jerry when they'd passed from his view.

"They're gone," Jerry said. "Went out the door leading to the street."

Clint turned and took a look.

"Maybe they're just the curious types," Jerry said.

"No," Clint said, "I got a feel for this kind of thing. They're interested, but it's not idle interest."

"Well," Jerry said, "maybe the sheriff will find something out tomorrow, or scare them off."

"Yeah," Clint said, "maybe."

"Anyway," Jerry said, "you got a big game tomorrow. You can't afford to be distracted."

"I know," Clint said. "I found that out today."

"So put those two jaspers out of your mind," Jerry said, "so you can concentrate on Gentleman Lou Teacher."

Clint raised his glass and said, "Here's to Gentleman Lou."

TWENTY-SEVEN

Julia Sacks went home to the ranch that night, not satisfied at all with the way things were going. She wondered if Burkett was getting some idea of robbing the game and keeping the money for himself. Actually, she wouldn't have minded that so much. If he was satisfied to take that money and leave town, she'd just find herself another man to satisfy her. That is, if he managed to kill her husband at the same time.

But what if he was intending to rob the game and leave Jerry alive? That wouldn't work at all. She needed Jerry to be dead, so she'd have the house and the money, and the businesses. Then she'd have her pick of men to satisfy her—maybe even younger men who'd be interested in helping a rich widow get over her husband's death.

Then she wondered about Clint Adams. Certainly not a younger man, but would he come around to console her when his friend was dead? After all, she was convinced it was only Jerry that kept Clint Adams from taking her right then and there on the pool table. The thought of it sent a ripple down her spine. Just thinking about going to bed with a man who had killed so many other men was exciting.

But first, Burkett had to take care of her husband, or nothing else could happen.

Clint was about to pack it in and go to his room when another man came up alongside him.

"Buy you a beer?" Fast Eddie asked.

"I was about to turn in."

"Aw, come on, one more," Eddie said with a big grin.

"Okay," Clint said. "One more."

"Bartender," Eddie called, and held up two fingers. Danny Troy nodded and brought them two beers.

"There ya go, gents."

"Thanks, Danny," Eddie said.

"Do you know Troy?" Clint asked.

"Know him?" Fast Eddie said. "Sure, I've known him a long time. Him and me spent a lot of time lookin' at each other across a pool table when we were younger."

"Is that a fact?" Clint asked. "He told me he played, but he didn't tell me how good he was."

"Oh, he was good," Eddie said. "Coulda been one of the best, but he just stopped playin'."

"Any idea why?"

"None," Eddie said. "He won't talk about it. Just gave it up and started tendin' bar. I was surprised when I walked in here and saw him."

"Coincidence, huh?"

"Big coincidence."

Clint looked down the bar at the busy bartender. Troy

seemed very comfortable where he was. Clint decided to ask Jerry some more questions about him later.

"So you got Big Lou tomorrow, huh?" Fast Eddie said.

"Looks like it."

"Think you can beat 'im?"

"I guess anybody can beat anybody on any given day," Clint said.

"I don't believe that," Eddie said.

"No?"

"I believe in talent," Fast Eddie said. "I believe the man—or lady—with the most talent will always win."

"So by that logic, you're going to beat Lady Eight Ball."

"Oh, yeah," Eddie said. "She's a decent enough player, but talent-wise she can't match up with me."

"Sounds like that's a match I should watch," Clint said.

"It might be interesting," Eddie said, "depending on who shoots first. So many times these games hinge on the break."

"You've got a hell of a break," Clint said. "Sounds like a sledgehammer."

"Thanks," Fast Eddie said. "I'll have to watch your match with Lou, just in case you and I end up facing each other."

"Now that would be interesting," Clint said.

Eddie regarded Clint quizzically for a few moments, then said, "I have to ask. Do you really think you have a chance to win?"

"By your logic, no," Clint said with hesitation, "but luckily I use my own logic, and whatever I get involved in, I always have a chance to win."

TWENTY-EIGHT

Clint woke the next morning feeling that he had held his own quite well yesterday. He believed he would have won his match even if Cue Ball hadn't thrown it.

He had managed to hold his own while both Gentleman Lou and Fast Eddie tried to intimidate him. Lou was trying to damage his confidence going into their match. Eddie had been planting a seed for later, in case they faced each other. But the fact that Fast Eddie had even tried to intimidate him meant the man knew Clint had a chance to beat Gentleman Lou.

And if Eddie was trying to mess with Clint's head, then he was legitimately worried about Clint as a potential opponent.

In trying to intimidate him, both Lou and Eddie had succeeded in bolstering Clint's confidence.

He had mixed feelings, however, about Antonia's match with Fast Eddie. If she beat Eddie, then Clint wouldn't have to face him. But if Eddie beat Antonia, then Clint wouldn't have to worry about the potential consequences of facing her.

He dressed and went downstairs for breakfast. He made a mental note to be sure to take dinner away from the hotel later that evening.

Antonia was playing first, so she wasn't in the dining room when Clint went there. He had a quick breakfast, because he wanted to go and watch her play Fast Eddie.

When he entered the room, Jerry spotted him and walked over.

"How's it going?"

"Eddie broke, sank a ball, and he's been at it ever since," Jerry said. "Lady Eight Ball may never get to the table."

Clint didn't know how he felt about that.

It was time for a rerack so Eddie came walking over to where Clint and Jerry were standing. Antonia was staring at the table, had not looked up at all when Clint entered.

"Table feels good this mornin'," Eddie said. "How you doin', Clint?"

"Fine, Eddie," Clint said. "How far have you gone?"

"I'm at—what, Jerry? Ninety?"

"Yup."

Eddie caressed his stick.

"Everythin' just feels good this mornin'," he said. "What can I tell you?"

"Your rack is ready," Clint said.

Eddie smiled at Clint, then walked back to the table and ran that rack as well. The score was now 105–0.

"Plenty of time," Jerry said. "Three more racks at least."

"Yeah," Clint said, "if he misses."

"He'll miss."

Clint looked at Jerry, who was staring at the table.

"How do you know?" Clint asked.

Jerry looked at Clint.

"Don't worry, there's no fix," he said. "I can just feel it. He's more arrogant than usual today. He's not playing to beat her as much as he's playing to show you he can beat her."

Clint watched as Eddie started to shoot again. He shot two more racks, bringing the score to 135–0. On the next rack he looked up at Clint and grinned just before breaking. The balls scattered all around the table. The 15 ball rolled toward the corner pocket but caught just a small piece of the corner, rattled around, and then stopped right there, hanging.

"There it is," Jerry said. "Her one chance."

Eddie's face was blank as he stepped away from the table, but Clint knew he was annoyed—or puzzled.

Antonia stepped up to the table and Lady Eight Ball began to shoot.

TWENTY-NINE

Clint put the chalk to his cue tip and watched as Jerry racked the balls for his match with Gentleman Lou. The door opened and Lou came walking in. Lou spotted Clint and walked over.

"Is it true?"

"Is what true?"

"Lady Eight Ball beat Eddie?"

"Oh, that," Clint said. "Yes, it's true."

"Geez, what happened?"

"Eddie missed."

"One miss?"

"That's all it takes, right?" Clint asked. "She stepped up to the table and that was it. Eddie never got back."

"Well," Lou said.

"You can't lose your concentration," Clint said. "Not even once. If you do, you're dead."

Lou hesitated a moment, then asked, "Are you talking about pool, or something else, Clint?"

Clint smiled.

"I believe it's time for us to lag for break," he said.

They stepped up, each struck their balls, and watched as they struck the far cushion, rolled back, bounced off the near cushion, and stopped.

Jerry stepped up and said, "It's close, but Clint Adams breaks."

Gentleman Lou stepped back and Clint waited while the balls were racked. Other players came in to watch. As he stared at the table, he realized that he could see each of his shots ahead of time. In fact, he could see six or seven shots ahead. And he didn't have to line them up, but—as with his gun—all he had to do was point, and the ball would go into the intended pocket. It really was the simplest thing.

Clint made his shots in machinelike fashion, with no pause. The sounds of balls striking balls, and then balls sinking into pockets, filled the room. He moved around the table crisply, executed the shot that he could see in his mind, and then moved on to the next one.

He was lining up his next shot when Jerry came over and placed a hand over his.

"What?" Clint said.

"It's over," Jerry said. "That's one hundred and fifty. You won."

Clint stood up straight and looked over at Gentleman Lou, who was still standing as he had been the whole time, with the blunt end of the stick on the floor. Only now the stick seemed to be holding him up.

"Clint Adams wins," Jerry announced. "If we can move along, the next match can begin."

Clint walked up to Lou and held out his hand. "Sorry you didn't get a chance to shoot," he said. "I was looking forward to watching you."

"That was . . ." Lou said, groping for a word. "Amazing."

"Thank you."

"Your concentration was . . . astounding. You didn't look up from the table once."

"I didn't have any reason to," Clint said as they walked to the door. "That's what caused Fast Eddie to lose."

"Exactly what?" Lou asked.

"Just before his final break, he had to look up at me and grin," Clint said. "Arrogance, and a lack of concentration."

"Well," Lou said, "I wasn't given a chance to exhibit either."

He continued on while Clint stopped and waited. Jerry Sacks got the next match started and Clint could hear the clack of balls as the door opened and closed.

"Happy?" Clint asked.

"Well . . ."

"What's wrong?"

"The odds, Clint," Jerry said. "What you did in there destroyed the odds for your next match."

"And my next match is against Antonia?"

"No," Jerry said. "Your next will be against whoever wins this match, that's going on now. Her next will be the winner of the next. Those will be played tonight. If the two of you win again, then you'll face each other in the final match tomorrow."

"I see."

"Relax the rest of the afternoon, come back tonight, after dinner. By then you'll know who your next opponent will be."

"Who's left?" Clint hadn't been keeping track.

"Nobody," Jerry said. "I'm pretty sure the final match

will be you and Antonia. And the way you shot today, you'll probably be favored."

"Well, that doesn't matter, does it?" Clint asked. "I mean, you just wanted me to win, right?"

"Well . . . yeah, that was the general idea," Jerry said, "but I did want to make some money on side bets."

"And I won too easily, is that it?"

"You did what I thought you'd do eventually," Jerry said. "You brought all your talent with a gun to bear on the pool table. Each of those balls became a bullet. And you didn't miss once."

"No," Clint said, "no, I didn't. It was . . . amazing to me, too. I mean, I wasn't even keeping count. When you stopped me, I had no idea I had sunk that many balls."

"Yeah," Jerry said, "we were all pretty amazed, especially poor Gentleman Lou. I think he was in shock."

"Yeah, he was, wasn't he?" Clint asked. "I can't say I'm really sorry about that, though."

"Let's go down and have a celebratory beer."

"What about the match going on?"

"They'll tell me who wins," Jerry said. "It doesn't really matter, does it? You and Lady Eight Ball will take care of the winners."

THIRTY

Word got around quickly that Clint and Lady Eight Ball
had won their matches. Davis and Tulley were in a smaller
saloon down the street, not wanting to be seen in the Alhambra anymore.

"Okay," Tulley said. "So how do we get Adams out of
the Alhambra and into the street?"

"I'm bettin' he'll get himself out of there."

"How?"

"He'll be wantin' to celebrate, and get out of that hotel at some point."

"We can't depend on that," Tulley said.

"Well, maybe we can figure out a way to get him out,
then," Davis said. "But right now we've got another problem."

"What problem?" Tulley asked.

Davis jerked his head. Tulley turned and saw that the
sheriff had entered the saloon, and was walking toward
them.

"Oh," he said.

"Let me do the talkin'."

When the sheriff reached the table, he said, "Boys."

"Sheriff," Davis said. "What can we do for you?"

"First," the lawman said, "your names."

"I'm Austin Davis, and this is my partner, Wilson Tulley."

"Partners in what?"

Davis spread his arms.

"In whatever work we can get."

"And what work brought you to Tucson?" Sheriff Lambert asked.

"Actually, Sheriff, we're just passin' through, and we heard about this big pool tournament. So we thought we'd stick around and see who wins."

"You really that interested in who wins?" Lambert asked.

Davis shrugged.

"Why not? It's pretty interesting, don't you think? To see if the Gunsmith can win?"

"So you know the Gunsmith is involved?"

"Who doesn't?" Davis asked. "It's all over town, ain't it?"

"Yeah, I guess it is," Lambert said, "but I'm hopin' that's as far as your interest in Clint Adams goes."

"Why else would we be interested?" Davis asked. He looked at Tulley, who just shrugged. "We're not gunmen, Sheriff, if that's what you're thinkin'. We're not after Clint Adams's reputation. That would be stupid."

"Yes, it would," Lambert said. "In fact, it would be suicidal."

"I don't disagree with you," Davis said, "and if there's one thing Tulley and me ain't, it's suicidal."

"I'm real glad to hear that, boys," Lambert said, "real glad."

"So you tell Adams he's got nothin' to fear from us," Davis said.

"You think he sent me here?"

"We saw you together last night," Davis said. "It was just a thought."

"You boys just remember what we talked about here," the sheriff said.

"Don't worry, Sheriff," Davis said, "we'll remember."

The sheriff nodded, and walked out.

Tulley started to speak but Davis cut him off with a wave. When he was sure the sheriff was gone, he said, "Go ahead."

"What do we do now, Austin?" Tulley asked.

"We don't change our plan at all," Davis said.

"Whataya mean? What plan?"

"We take Adams out, like we planned."

"The sheriff's gonna know it was us."

"No, he ain't," Davis said. "He warned us off. He'll never believe it was us when Adams turns up dead."

"But how do we get to Adams?" Tulley asked.

"You're right, we didn't have a plan," Davis said, "but I've got one now. The sheriff gave it to me."

"What? How did he do that?"

"Why don't you get us a couple of more beers, Wilson," Davis said, "and I'll tell you all about it."

"Okay," Tulley said, "but I hope this is a good plan, Austin."

"Don't worry," Davis said. "It is."

THIRTY-ONE

"What's going on, Frank?" Julia Sacks demanded.

Burkett looked back at Julia. They were sitting in her living room. She'd sent for him, certain that her husband would still be in town.

"You sure your husband isn't gonna come back?" Burkett asked.

"If he does," she said, "you can kill him today. But no, he won't be back."

"How about a drink, babe?"

She crossed her arms and glared at him.

"I didn't call you here for a drink, or for sex," she said. "Why the hell isn't my husband dead yet? Why haven't you robbed that game?"

Burkett sat down.

"And where the hell are the men you promised me?" she added.

"I changed my mind," he said, crossing his leg over his knee.

"You what?"

"Changed my mind."

"You're not going to kill him?"

"No, I am," he said. "And I'm gonna rob the game. I'm just not gonna need any help to do it."

"And how do you figure to do that?"

"I could explain better with a drink in my hand," Burkett said, "and without you lookin' over me. How about it?"

She relented, walked to a sideboard, and poured two brandies. She handed him one, then sat across from him with the other.

"All right," she said. "I'm waiting to hear this great plan of yours."

He sipped his brandy and said, "It's very simple . . ."

"It's real simple," Austin Davis said after he'd finished telling Wilson Tulley his plan to kill Clint Adams.

"And you think this is gonna work?"

"Why not?"

"We send him a message to meet us and sign the sheriff's name?"

"Right."

"Then bushwhack him."

"Right again."

Tulley looked into his drink.

"What's wrong?" Davis asked.

"It's too simple."

"You got a better idea?"

"No."

"Then get some paper and pencil from the bartender, and we'll write the note."

"Who's gonna write it?" Tulley asked.

"I am."

"And who's gonna deliver it?" Suspiciously now.

"You are."

"Why doesn't that surprise me?"

"That's your plan?" Julia asked.

"That's it."

She thought a moment. He stood up and went to get himself another glass of brandy. He held the decanter out to her, but she shook her head. He returned to the sofa and waited.

"I can see where that would get you the money from the tournament," she said finally, "but how about killing my husband?"

"Oh, I can do that, too," he said, "but later."

"How much later?"

"Not much," he said. "You'll be happy with the results, Julia. I guarantee it."

"I better be."

"And I won't have to share the money with anyone," he added.

"No," she said, "if your plan works, it's all yours. And so am I."

"Right," he said, looking at her over the rim of his glass, "so are you."

THIRTY-TWO

Clint couldn't find Antonia.

He had the feeling Lady Eight Ball was avoiding him. Apparently, she'd already figured out that it would be the two of them in the finals. And the only way she could handle it was to stay away from him.

Well, that was okay. Neither of them would be distracted.

He was walking through the lobby when the desk clerk called, "Mr. Adams."

"Yes?"

"Note for you, sir."

Clint approached the desk. The clerk handed him a simple piece of paper, written on with a pencil.

"Thanks."

"Of course, sir."

Clint walked away from the desk, unfolded the note, read it. He refolded it and walked back to the desk.

"Who delivered this?" he asked.

"I don't know, sir," the clerk said. "I left the desk for a moment, and when I came back, it was here."

"When?"

"Just a few minutes ago."

Clint turned and walked out onto the boardwalk, looked both ways. There was no sign of the sheriff. Maybe he'd sent the note with a deputy?

He took the note out and read it again.

Need your help. Please meet me at the corner of South Street and Fourth, in front of the hardware store, at seven p.m. It was signed: *The Sheriff.*

He folded the note and put it in his pocket. He still had an hour before his appointment.

Wilson Tulley watched from across the street, saw Clint Adams read the note and put it in his pocket. Whether or not he showed up for the meeting with the sheriff remained to be seen. All Tulley needed to do now was tell Davis the note had been delivered, and read.

He waited for Clint Adams to turn his back, then slipped from his hiding place.

Clint stopped a block from the corner of South and Fourth. It was ten minutes to seven. The moon was high, but not full, casting enough shadows for his purposes. Also casting enough light. He walked the remaining block in the shadows.

He saw one man in a doorway, across the street. His bet was there was at least one more man on a rooftop directly above him. Once he crossed the street and stood in front of the hardware store, he'd be spotlighted not only by the moon, but by a streetlamp. They'd have him in a cross fire.

But that was if he went and stood on that corner.

* * *

Austin Davis kept his eyes on the well-lit corner from the rooftop across the street, his hands tightening on his rifle. Tulley was in a doorway across from him. All Adams had to do was cross the street and he'd be dead meat.

Davis was a good shot with a rifle. He couldn't miss from where he was.

Tulley was nervous.

From where he was, he could see the corner, but he could not see his partner up on the roof. What if something had happened and Davis wasn't there? That would leave Tulley alone against the Gunsmith, and that wasn't something he had signed up for.

He decided he was going to wait for the first shot to come from Davis. Once he fired from the roof and Tulley knew he was there, then he'd open fire as well.

To Clint, it was a simple case of picking the rooftop he himself would have chosen. Once he chose it, he saw there was no access from outside. He had to climb to a lower roof nearby, climb to a second roof, and then finally make his way up to the third one. A man with a rifle could simply toss the rifle up ahead of him each time. Clint was wearing his holster, had no rifle, which was good, because he had to move quietly.

He hoisted himself up to the roof in question, paused to make sure he'd chosen the right one. He had. There was a man by the edge of the roof with a rifle. His back was to Clint, who had to haul himself the rest of the way up as quietly as he could.

He didn't count on the rooftop being covered with

gravel. As soon as his boots touched on the rooftop, the gravel crunched beneath his feet.

The man with the rifle whirled quickly and Clint had no choice. As the rifle barrel came around, he drew and fired. His bullet struck the man in the chest. The rifle flew from his hands and off the roof, and the man followed. The bullet had shoved him back against the parapet, and he flipped over. He must have been dead already, though, because he made no noise as he fell.

Only when he landed.

Across the street Tulley heard the shot, and heard the body hit the street with a sound like wet cement. He wasn't sure what it was, but the sound did draw him out of his hiding place. Immediately he felt the barrel of a gun being shoved into his ear.

"You're under arrest, friend," Sheriff Lambert said, relieving Tulley of his gun.

THIRTY-THREE

"I had no choice but to shoot," Clint told the sheriff later, "and then he just fell over the edge."

"I believe you, Clint," Lambert said. "Hey, you came to me with this instead of handling it yourself. That says a lot."

"Thanks."

"Have a seat."

Clint sat in front of the sheriff's desk, accepted a mug of coffee. The sheriff went around and sat behind his desk, then pulled a bottle of whiskey from a drawer.

"Taste?" he asked.

"Yes, thanks."

The sheriff topped off both of their coffees with whiskey, then put the bottle away.

"What made you come to me with that note?" he asked.

"It just didn't sound like you," Clint said. "First, it said 'please.' "

"What? I'm not polite?"

"Lawman types usually expect people to do what they say," Clint said, "or even what they ask. Also, asking me to meet you on some street corner? At night? Not likely. A badge would make much too easy a target."

"Well, the dead man is Austin Davis, a drifter who came into town a few days ago. His partner in the cell is Wilson Tulley, and I don't know if I can hold him."

"Why not?"

"He didn't do anything."

"He was waiting to bushwhack me."

"We know that, but a judge would say he didn't do anything, never even fired a shot. He could have been an innocent bystander."

"So you're going to cut him loose?"

"Not right away," the sheriff said. "I'll keep him overnight, see if he confesses. If not, then I might have to let him leave. I'll see that he rides out of town."

"If he decides to try and get revenge, or just make another try at me, I can't guarantee he won't end up dead," Clint said.

"I understand that," Lambert said. "And I'll let you know before I let him go, so you'll be aware."

"Thanks."

Clint finished his whiskey-laced coffee and stood up.

"Mind if I talk to him before I go?"

"Go ahead," the sheriff said, "but leave me your gun."

Clint took his gun from his holster and handed it to the sheriff, who stuck it in a drawer.

Clint walked into the cell block. There were three cells, only one inhabited. As he approached, Wilson Tulley lifted his head from his hands and looked up.

"It wasn't my idea," he said, holding his hands out.

"Take it easy," Clint said. "I don't have a gun. Whose idea was it?"

"It was Austin's," Tulley said. "He wanted to rob that big game that's goin' on, but he figured we should get rid of you first."

"So it wasn't just a try at me," Clint said. "You fellas wanted to take off the game?"

"That's right."

"And nobody else was involved?"

"No, just us," Tulley said. "Really, Mr. Adams, it wasn't my idea."

"I know, you said that."

"Ya gotta lemme go, Mr. Adams," Tulley said. "I'll leave town, promise."

"That's not my decision," Clint said. "It's up to the sheriff."

"But you'll talk to him for me?"

Clint laughed.

"Not a chance," he said. "You're on your own."

Clint walked back out to the office, retrieved his gun from Sheriff Lambert.

"What were you thinkin'?" Lambert asked.

"I was just wondering if this was part of something bigger," he said.

"Like what?"

"He says he and his partner were going to rob the game, but didn't want to do it while I was there."

"Sacks has no security set up, does he?"

"Not that I know of," Clint said, "but that's something I should've asked before."

"Not your job," the sheriff said. "You're one of the players."

"I know," Clint said, "but I still should have asked about it."

Clint headed for the door.

"Where are you going?" Lambert asked.

"I'm going to ask now."

THIRTY-FOUR

Clint found Jerry Sacks having a steak in the hotel dining room. He was eating alone.

"Clint, have a seat," Jerry said.

"No, I was going to eat somewhere else tonight," Clint said.

"You eat on the house here, remember?" Jerry asked.

"Yeah, there is that," Clint said. "Okay." He pulled out a chair and sat, ordered a steak dinner. "By the way, how did you get the hotel to agree to feed us all for free?"

Jerry leaned forward and confessed, "I own the joint."

"The hotel and the saloon?"

"The whole shebang."

"But you told all the pool players that you didn't own the place."

"It's not generally known."

"Okay. I'll keep it to myself."

"Thanks. Where you been?"

"Getting shot at," Clint said. "Well, almost."

Jerry stared at Clint.

"You seem pretty calm for somebody who got shot at," he said.

"It's nothing new for me," Clint said. "Besides, I said almost."

He told Jerry what happened, didn't stop talking even when his dinner came.

"Which brings me to a question I should have asked you from the beginning."

"What have I done about security?" Jerry asked.

"Exactly."

"I do have somebody taking care of security, Clint," Jerry said. "I'm not stupid."

"I didn't say you were," Clint said, "I'm just asking because I haven't seen anybody . . ."

"Well, that just shows you how good he is," Jerry said. "I'll introduce you after we finish eating. How's that?"

"Sounds good."

"So what's the sheriff gonna do with the one you caught?"

"Let him go if he doesn't confess," Clint said. "He never fired a shot."

"But he would have."

"Can't send him to prison for that."

"You could kill him," Jerry suggested.

"I don't kill anyone who's not trying to kill me," Clint told him.

"Sorry," Jerry said, raising his hands. "I didn't mean anything by it.'

They finished dinner and pondered dessert.

"What's going on upstairs?" Clint asked.

"Play's over for the day. We got two matches tomorrow. You and Antonia are playing guys who only got through because of the draw."

"You mean because I happened to play Lou and she happened to play Fast Eddie. How did four of the best players end up playing each other like that, Jerry?"

"Hey," Jerry said, "I told you no more funny business. I only did that in the first round."

"I hope you stick to that, Jerry."

"Hey, my word is my word. You wanna get dessert or not? I got a cook that combines peach and blueberry in a great pie. Afterward, I'll introduce you to my security guy."

"Peach and blueberry together?"

"The blueberries dye the peaches blue. It's great."

"Well," Clint said, since his favorite pie was peach, "I'll give it a try."

The peach and blueberry pie was so good, Clint had a second piece.

"That's the best dessert I've ever tasted," he said. "My compliments to the cook."

"I'll tell him."

They had another pot of coffee and then had to stop. They were both as full as they could get.

As they walked into the lobby, Clint asked, "Where's your security guy now that no game is going on?"

"He's in my office, with the safe," Jerry said.

"Does he have the combination?"

"Only I have the combination," Jerry said. "Come on."

They walked to the rear of the lobby and down a hall to a closed door. Jerry opened it and let Clint enter first. The man inside got to his feet when he saw Clint, then relaxed when he saw Jerry.

"Clint," Jerry said. "I want you to meet my security man, Frank Burkett."

THIRTY-FIVE

Clint shook hands with the big, dark-haired man. He had a firm grip, lots of wiry black hair on the back of his hand.

"Glad to meet you."

"You're pretty good at this," Clint said. "I didn't notice you."

"I don't stand out," Burkett said. "See, I'm big and ugly. People either don't look at me, or don't wanna look at me."

Well, Clint wasn't going to argue with the man. He was big, and he did look kind of homely.

"Excuse me for asking," Clint said to Jerry, "but is this it? I mean, one man?"

"There's only one safe," Jerry said, "and the prize money stays in there until somebody wins."

"What about the side bets?"

"The money doesn't exchange hands right away," Jerry said. "So nobody who's playing has any real money on them—unless you're carrying a bundle?"

"I'm not," Clint assured him.

"So most of the money is in there," Jerry said, indicating his safe, "and Frank sits on it."

Clint studied Burkett for a moment.

"Satisfied?" Jerry asked.

"Sure," Clint said. "Nice meeting you, Frank."

"Same here, Adams."

After Jerry and Clint had left the room, Clint commented, "Frank seems more like a payroll guard than a security man."

"Frank don't much mind what he's called as long as he gets paid, Clint. Don't worry so much. Just watch your back from now on—just in case those guys were after you."

"I always watch my back, Jerry," Clint said. "I don't know anybody else who would do as good a job at it. Listen, have you seen Antonia this evening?"

"As a matter of fact, no. I was wondering where she was. You two have a spat?"

"No, but I think she's avoiding me," Clint said.

"She's probably just getting herself ready to play against you," Jerry said. "You know, getting herself in the right frame of mind."

"Yeah, you're probably right."

"You should do the same," Jerry said. "Have a drink and turn in."

"I'll do that," Clint said. "See you tomorrow, Jerry."

"You should win tomorrow, Clint," Jerry said. "If you show up in the right frame of mind also. Understand?"

"Sure, Jerry. I understand."

Clint went to the saloon. He might have gone to another saloon just to get out of the Alhambra, but the last time he went out, somebody tried to shoot him.

He went to the bar and asked Danny Troy for a beer.

"Heard you're playin' for all the money tomorrow," Troy said.

"Looks like it."

"Against the lady. She musta got real lucky against Fast Eddie."

"Or she played better."

"Yeah, right. She gonna play better than you tomorrow, Clint?"

"She might."

"Yeah, like I got a chance of outshootin' you with a gun."

"Seen the lady tonight, Danny?"

"Nope, she hasn't been in here."

Clint looked around. The saloon seemed empty.

"What about the other players?"

"What other players?" Troy asked. "They all lost, right? They left town."

"Not interested in seeing who won?"

Troy shrugged.

"Maybe some of them are in their rooms, and they'll show up to watch tomorrow."

"Maybe."

"Maybe I'll ask Mr. Sacks if I can watch, too," Troy said. "I'm kinda curious."

"Watching might get you back in the mood for playing, Danny," Clint said. "You want to take that chance?"

Troy grinned and said, "I just might take that chance, Clint."

THIRTY-SIX

Clint woke the next morning hoping that people were through plotting to shoot him. He wondered what would have happened if Davis and Tulley had succeeded in killing him. That would have left Antonia without an opponent.

Jerry Sacks wouldn't have turned the prize money over to her just like that. He probably would have made her play either Gentleman Lou, or Fast Eddie. If that was the case, then the three of them stood to gain from having Clint shot. What if Austin Davis had taken a payoff to do just that, but didn't tell Tulley about it?

Jerry was right last night. Clint was going to have to watch his back very closely.

Breakfast in the dining room again. He was getting real tired of that place. When this was all over, he was going to find another restaurant in town—just before he left.

Over a quick ham-and-egg breakfast he wondered what would happen between Jerry and his wife. Should he tell Jerry how his wife had tried to sleep with him behind his back? No, his experience with telling friends that was that he ended up losing a friend. Nobody likes hearing that kind of thing about his wife.

He finished his coffee and headed upstairs.

Antonia awoke, realized for the first time in her life she was nervous about something. If she beat Clint this morning, she'd be on top. Nobody'd be able to take that away from her. Lady Eight Ball would be taken seriously from now on.

She got dressed and went out to have breakfast somewhere else. She didn't want to run into Clint. She'd been avoiding him ever since they found out they were going to play each other.

Frank Burkett sat in Jerry Sacks's office, staring at the safe. It sure would be easy if he had the combination. He could open it and take off with the money, and never look back.

However, killing Jerry Sacks had a certain appeal— and might just be necessary. Burkett was a homely man, but here he was fucking Sacks's beautiful wife because she couldn't get it at home. He would love for Sacks to know about that before he left town. But if he told Sacks that—*and* stole the money—he'd have no choice but to kill him before he left.

He had his hands flat on the top of Sacks's desk. He wondered if the man would be foolish enough to have the combination of the safe written down on a piece of paper somewhere in the desk.

He got up, went to the office door, and locked it. He didn't want anyone walking in on him while he was looking through the desk, least of all Jerry Sacks. This way Sacks would have to use his key, and that would be enough of a warning.

Frank went back behind the desk and started going through the drawers.

Julia was sitting at home, wondering if Frank Burkett was smarter than she thought he was.

In the beginning she'd chosen Burkett for several reasons. One, she didn't think he was very smart. Two, he worked for her husband. Three, he was so homely she thought he'd be easy to seduce. And four, he was a big man. She imagined he would be big all over, and she was right. She just hadn't figured his penis to be big *and* ugly.

Nevertheless, she was starting to wonder if her number one reason had been wrong. Was he smart enough to steal the money and take off, keeping it for himself without killing Jerry? She didn't care if he kept the money. That was part of the plan. But the part of the plan that was most important to her was killing her husband.

She was all set for Jerry to be dead by the time this whole pool thing was over. If Burkett ran out on her without doing it, she was going to have to kill Jerry herself.

There was enough money at stake for her to do it, if she had to.

THIRTY-SEVEN

Clint arrived before Antonia, found Jerry Sacks and a few other curious players waiting. Gentleman Lou and Fast Eddie were not among the curious. They were very unhappy men who had left town already.

"How'd you sleep?" Jerry asked.

"Like a baby."

"Excellent. I'm looking forward to a good match between the two of you."

"So am I."

Clint stepped up to the table and began to practice his lag for break.

When Antonia entered, she drew every eye as she was wearing a shirt, trousers, and a belt tightly cinched at the waist. It made her rear end very evident, and it would be even more so whenever she bent over to shoot.

Clint realized she was pulling out every weapon she had. The shirt was also tight, making the thrust of her large breasts seem even larger.

"Lag for break," Jerry said.

Clint and Antonia stood side by side and struck their respective balls. They hit the opposite cushion, came back, struck the near cushion, and everyone watched them as they rolled, slowed, and finally stopped.

Clint and Antonia looked at each other. It was close.

Jerry stepped to the table and examined the balls.

"I can't tell," he said after a few moments. "You'll have to do it again."

Clint and Antonia moved their balls, struck them again. It was a replay. The balls hit both cushions, rolled to a stop.

"Close again," Jerry said, "but this time I call it for Clint Adams."

"No," Antonia said.

"What?" Jerry asked.

"I don't accept that," she said. "To me it looks like my ball is closer. And he's playing for you. We need an impartial third party."

They all looked around the room.

"Pick somebody," Jerry said.

"Everybody in here has a bet going," she said. "It has to be somebody from outside the room."

"Like who?" Jerry asked.

"Anybody from the saloon," Clint suggested.

"Why don't you try again?" Jerry asked.

"No," she said, "I choose the bartender from the saloon."

"Which one?" Jerry asked.

"I don't care," she said. "Whichever one is working now."

"All right," Jerry said. "I'll go and get him."

Jerry left the room. Clint leaned over to Antonia.

"The bartender works for Jerry," he said.

"That's okay," she said. "It probably means he doesn't like him."

"You're probably right."

They looked down at the two balls.

"Still looks even to me," he said.

"No," she said, "mine's slightly ahead. If you were a gentleman, you'd let me shoot first."

"I might never get to the table, then," he said. "I think I'll put my faith in the bartender. After all, there's a lot of money at stake."

"Yes, there is," she said.

After another five minutes the spectators began to get restless. There were about six men watching. Not all of them had been players in the game. Some of them were armed. Clint started to wonder who they were when the door opened and Jerry entered leading Danny Troy.

"Okay," he said to Antonia. "Here's the bartender."

"Hello, ma'am," Troy said. "Sir."

"Hello," Clint said.

"Hi," Antonia said.

"Okay," Jerry said. "They lagged for break. Who won?"

Clint and Antonia were no longer standing by the table.

"Whose ball is whose?" Troy asked.

"That doesn't matter," Antonia said before Jerry could answer. "Just tell us which ball is the winner."

Troy stepped up to the table, leaned over, and looked down at the balls. Antonia had shot the cue ball, while Clint had shot the 13.

Troy straightened up.

"Well?" Jerry asked.

"It's real close," Troy said, "but I say the cue ball wins."

"Lady Eight Ball breaks!" Jerry announced.

THIRTY-EIGHT

Lady Eight Ball stepped up to the table and began to shoot. She moved slowly and methodically. The sounds of clacking balls filled the room, along with the sounds of the balls falling into the holes. Little by little, as she moved along, the sounds got harder, faster, the balls snapped into the holes rather than fell.

After the fourth rack, Jerry leaned into Clint and said, "She's on fire."

"Looks like it," Clint said, leaning on his stick.

"There's a long way to go, though."

After the fifth rack, she was halfway there.

"We might be in trouble," Jerry said.

"No," Clint said.

"Why?"

"She'll look up," Clint said. "Eventually, she'll look up at me to see how I'm taking this."

"And?"

"And at that moment, she'll miss."

"But when will that be?" Jerry asked.

Clint shrugged.

"What if she looks up at you on the last ball?" Jerry asked.

"Well, then," Clint said, "we may be in trouble."

In Jerry's office, Frank Burkett sat back in the desk chair and shook his head. It was too much to hope for that the safe combination would be written down on a slip of paper in the desk. Jerry Sacks obviously had it memorized.

The safe wasn't going to be opened until he came down to get the prize money and present it to the winner.

And Frank would be waiting.

Julia checked the time. She knew the final match would be going on now. That meant that sometime in the afternoon Jerry would be opening the safe and retrieving the prize money.

She pulled out the drawer of her dressing table and removed a small revolver. She stuck it into a drawstring purse and ran downstairs. She wanted to get to town to be there when the safe was opened.

"One-oh-five to nothing," Jerry announced. "Rack number eight coming up."

Clint stood by, leaning on his stick, watching intently. The first time Antonia looked up, he wanted her to see his eyes.

Jerry racked the balls for Antonia, and she kept staring at the table. She knew if she looked up, she'd be lost. Her concentration had to be complete. When he lifted the rack, she struck the cue ball as hard as she could. The 15 ball shot into the corner pocket like a bullet.

She was in motion again.

Clint had to admit she was beautiful moving around the table. The men watching didn't know where to look, at her breasts, her butt, or the balls on the table. She was distracting everyone in the room—everyone but Clint.

Oh, his attention was on her, but his concentration was there. As soon as she looked at him, he knew he'd have her. And if she never looked at him? Well, so what? He'd lose the tournament. Jerry Sacks would lose some money. And so would he. But he'd lost money before. Many times. Why not one more time?

What was the difference?

Jerry looked over at Clint, who was watching Antonia run another rack on the table. He was thinking about the prize money in the safe, and all the side bet money he would lose if Antonia won. It wouldn't break him, not at all. But there was more than money at stake here. After all, Clint represented him.

Antonia was beautiful, though, moving around the table.

THIRTY-NINE

Burkett looked up when the door opened. Somebody with a key. It had to be Jerry Sacks, but it wasn't.

"Julia!" he said. "What are you doing here?"

"I want to be here when the safe is opened," she said. "I want to be here when you do it."

Burkett laughed.

"You don't trust me," he said.

"Well," she said, "you *are* a man."

"That's true," he said. After all, hadn't he been thinking about running out on her?

"Do you know who's winning?" she asked.

"I haven't heard a word."

She walked to the desk and sat down.

"I'll wait with you."

"What are you going to say to your husband when he sees you here?" he asked.

She smiled and said, "I'm going to say good-bye."

* * *

"One thirty-five to nothing," Jerry announced. "This could be the final rack."

Clint was enjoying himself. Antonia had waited a long time for this. It was her chance to command respect for more than how she looked.

Jerry came over and stood by Clint.

"She's not gonna miss," he said.

"I know."

"She's gonna win."

"I know."

Jerry looked at Clint.

"You don't mind?"

"Do you know what it came down to, Jerry?"

"What?"

"She wanted it more than anyone else. It's about more than money to her."

There were five balls left. She walked around the table. Sank one. Four left.

"Jesus," Jerry said. "You're never gonna get to the table."

"I know."

Another ball went into a pocket. Three left.

"You knew she was gonna win, didn't you?"

"No," Clint said, "I didn't know. But I'm not surprised."

"You're gonna lose your five hundred dollars."

"That's okay. You're going to lose a lot more than that, aren't you?"

"It won't break me," Jerry said. "I'm just sorry I couldn't play myself."

"I did the best I could," Clint said.

"You did more than that," Jerry said. "If Troy had picked your ball—"

"You brought him up here to pick my ball, didn't you?" Clint asked.

"Uh, well—"

"Only you forgot to tell him which one was mine."

"Actually," Jerry said, "I forgot which one was yours, until we got back here. Then it was too late."

"So he had a fifty-fifty chance of being right," Clint said.

"And then maybe you would've kept Antonia off the table, instead of the other way around."

Clunk.

Two left.

"Well," Jerry said, looking at the table, "she could still miss."

"Yes, she could."

"But she won't, will she?"

"No," Clint said. "She's locked in."

Clunk.

One left.

"She's pretty good," Jerry said, holding his arms across his chest.

"Yeah, she is," Clint said.

"Five ball, corner pocket," Antonia said.

She lined it up and shot it into the pocket with a loud bang. Then and only then did she look up at Clint and smile.

"Lady Eight Ball wins!" Jerry announced, and the spectators applauded.

FORTY

"Is the poker game over?" Clint asked Jerry.

"No, it's down to two players."

"I'll go and watch while you take Antonia to your office and pay her off."

"Okay. I'll see you later."

Antonia walked over to Clint and he shook her hand.

"I'm proud of you," he said.

"I knew if I ever looked up at you, I'd miss," she said.

"But you didn't," he said. "You kept your concentration."

"Yeah, I did."

"Go get paid off."

"You're not coming?"

"I'll see you after," he said. "We'll do something to celebrate."

She touched his arm and said, "And I know what. I owe you an apology, too."

"You did what you had to do to win, Antonia," Clint said. "Go get your reward."

She kissed him hastily on the cheek and said, "See you later."

She turned and followed Jerry out of the room.

Downstairs Jerry opened the door to the office and told Antonia, "After you."

She entered the room and he came in behind her. He stopped short when he saw Julia sitting across from Frank Burkett.

"Frank," he said, "you're not supposed to let anyone in here."

"I didn't let her in," Burkett said. "She had her own key."

Jerry frowned at his wife.

"She's not supposed to have a key," he said.

"I had one made up," she said with a smile.

"This is your wife?" Antonia asked.

"Yes," Jerry said. "Julia, this is Antonia Delaware. Lady Eight Ball. She won the tournament."

"Congratulations," Julia said, and shot Lady Eight Ball in the chest.

"Jesus!" Jerry said.

Burkett stood and pointed his gun at Jerry.

"Time to open the safe."

FORTY-ONE

Clint watched as the two men sent money back and forth across the table. They were evenly matched as far as talent went.

Neither had any.

He grew bored within minutes and decided to go down to the saloon for a beer instead, and wait for Antonia there. Maybe even talk with Danny Troy. Odd that a former player, who had not picked up a stick for years, had had such an effect on the outcome of the final game.

"I won't."

"Make him, Frank," Julia said.

"You should have waited for him to open it before you got trigger happy, Julia," Burkett said.

"You two?" Jerry asked. "Together?"

"Why not, Jerry?" she asked. "Frank's a man. He gives me what I want."

"Money? Can he give you that, Julia? Because that's what you want."

"And that's what I'm going to have, dear husband," she said.

"Don't shoot him!" Burkett said.

"I'm not stupid, Frank," she said. "Get him to open the safe."

At that point Antonia moaned and moved on the floor. Burkett walked over to her and pointed his gun at her head.

"Open the safe, or I'll kill her," he said.

Jerry looked at Burkett, Julia, Antonia, and then at the safe.

"Don't you give him my money, Sacks," Antonia said.

"Shut up, bitch!" Julia said.

"Make up your mind, Jerry," Burkett said. "Open the safe or watch her die."

"And then you'll die," Jerry said.

"You won't be here to see it," Burkett said. "After I kill her, I'll kill you."

"Come on, Jerry," Julia said. "The money in the safe won't break you."

He glared at her, then looked at Frank Burkett.

"Why would you do this, Frank?" he asked. "Just for her?"

"For money, Sacks," Burkett said. "For money. What else?"

"This prize money won't last you forever," Jerry said.

"It'll last long enough," Burkett said. "Open the safe. Now!"

Julia watched as Jerry knelt down in front of the safe. Two hundred thousand was a good payoff, but she had much more at stake. He had no idea that opening that safe would be the last thing he'd ever do.

She realized, suddenly, that she really had never needed Frank Burkett at all. She could have done this herself. It had been easy to shoot the bitch, and should be just as easy to shoot her husband. The problem now was Frank Burkett. If she wanted to get rid of him, she was going to have to wait for her chance, since he was also armed.

Right now she'd go along with the plan, but later . . .

Clint was drinking his beer and talking pool with Danny Troy when they all heard the shot.

"What the—" Troy said.

Clint stood up straight.

"Where did that come from?"

"Sounded like inside the building," Troy said. "Maybe the office?"

"Damn it!" Clint said. He put his beer down so fast it spilled, but he was already racing across the floor to the office. When he got to the door, he found it locked. Troy came up behind him.

"Who's got the key?" he demanded.

"The boss is supposed to have the only key."

"We'll have to break it down. Lend me a shoulder."

They both put their shoulders to the door and it opened with the sound of cracking wood.

"Jesus," Troy said. On the floor were both Antonia Delaware and Jerry Sacks. The safe was open and the prize money was gone.

And so was Frank Burkett.

FORTY-TWO

Jerry Sacks was dead.

Antonia was alive.

They sent for the sheriff and the doctor. Meanwhile, Clint looked for another way out, found a back door that led to an alley behind the building. When he got back inside, the sheriff was there.

"Looks like he had a horse out back," Clint said. "He must have planned this. It wasn't a spur-of-the-moment thing."

"Damn it, poor Jerry," the sheriff said.

The doctor arrived then, bent to examine both bodies.

"She gonna make it, Doc?" the Sheriff asked.

"I don't know," the older man said. "We'll have to take her to my office. I can tell ya one thing for sure, though."

"What's that?" Clint asked.

"These folks were shot with different guns. Him a large caliber, her a small."

The sheriff looked at Clint.

"I only heard one shot," Clint said.

"So did I," Troy added from the sidelines.

Other customers standing around the office door nodded their agreement.

"I need some help getting the lady to my office," the doctor said.

He had more than enough volunteers.

"And to take Mr. Sacks to the undertaker's," he added.

There weren't so many volunteers for that, so the sheriff had to pick out a few extra hands.

While the bodies were being moved, a small man came up and said to the sheriff, "I got somethin' ta tell ya, Sheriff."

"What's that?"

"I, uh, saw a woman go into the office."

"When?"

"Oh, a couple of hours ago."

"Do you know who she was?"

"No, sir, but she was real pretty," the man said. "Blonde."

"Can you tell us anything else?" Clint asked.

"One thing," the man said.

"What?" the sheriff asked.

"She opened the door with a key."

Clint looked at Sheriff Lambert and said, "Julia!"

FORTY-THREE

As they rode out to the Sacks ranch, Clint told the sheriff how Julia had tried to seduce him.

"Just because she wanted to cheat on her husband doesn't make her a killer," Lambert said.

"Antonia was shot with a small gun—a woman's gun. The shot wasn't even heard, that's how small it was. Burkett shot Jerry with his gun."

"Burkett's a pretty ugly guy," Lambert said. "You think him and Mrs. Sacks . . ."

"If it was all about money, why not?" Clint asked. "Besides, if Julia needed sex, she'd probably take it from anybody."

The sheriff looked morose. Was he wondering why she had never come on to him? Clint shook his head. No, he was probably wondering how he was going to arrest a woman.

"Why do you think Burkett will be at the ranch?" he asked.

"Because that's where his final payoff will come from," Clint said.

"But doesn't he know that's where we'll look?" the sheriff asked.

"That depends on what part of his body he's thinking with," Clint said.

At the ranch Julia entered the house ahead of Burkett, who was taking care of the horses. She had two choices. Take him to bed, or kill him. The problem was, watching him kill her husband had excited her. She needed to be taken to bed. The other problem was the law, and Clint Adams would probably be coming here after they found the bodies of Jerry and the bitch, Antonia.

Burkett came into the house, slamming the door behind him.

"Where's your money?" she asked.

"I hid it."

"From me?"

"From anybody. What are you doing?"

"Trying to decide whether to fuck you, or kill you," she said.

"I vote for fuck," he said. "What do we do if the law comes here?"

"That's easy," she said. "We alibi each other, say we were in bed together the whole time."

"And if they don't believe us?"

"They can't prove otherwise," she said, approaching him. She put one hand on his chest and the other between his legs. "Now take me upstairs and give me this monster of yours."

* * *

They had half an hour. Burkett had Julia on her hands and knees and was taking her roughly from behind when they heard somebody in the house. He grabbed for his gun.

"Easy, lover," she said. "I told you, they can't prove anything."

"Adams saw me in the office," he said. "I was on guard."

"And when Jerry and Lady Eight Ball came down to get her prize, he sent you away. You were finished guarding the safe, and you don't know what happened after you left."

"And what if somebody saw you come in?"

"There's a back way out, isn't there?" she said.

He was still inside her. She leaned forward so that his huge cock slid out of her, then reached behind, took hold of him, and stroked him.

"Come on, baby," she said. "Keep pumping."

"What if they walk in on us?" he asked.

"That'll be their problem," she said. She slid back, taking him inside again with a sigh. "Fuck me, baby."

"You're a crazy bitch, Julia," he said.

Clint entered the house, gun in hand, and stopped to listen. He waited for the sheriff to join him.

"Two horses in the barn, look like they been rode hard."

"They're here," Clint said. "I can hear them."

"Where are they?"

"Listen."

They stood still and listened. They could hear a man and a woman upstairs, grunting and crying out.

"Damn," Lambert said. "That ain't somethin' I wanna see."

"But it's something they want us to see," Clint said.

"I guess we better go on up," Lambert said.

"No, I've got a better idea," Clint said.

"What's that?"

"Let's wait for them to come to us."

FORTY-FOUR

"What's goin' on?" Burkett asked.

He was leaning over Julia, having just exploded inside her. They were both trying to catch their breaths.

"I'm not sure," she said. "I know I heard them down there."

He slid out of her and stumbled off the bed, grabbing his gun.

"I'm gonna find out," he said.

"Like that?" she asked.

He looked down at himself.

"Put on your clothes, Frank." She pulled on a robe. "In fact, let me go down first."

"Hey, wait—"

"Don't worry," she said. "I'll take care of them until you come down."

Clint and Sheriff Lambert were sitting on the sofa when Julia came down. She was wearing a robe, which was pulled down on one side to reveal one creamy shoulder and part of a full breast.

"Thank God you're here," she said, running to Clint. She clung to him. "H-He said he killed Jerry, and then he—he raped me."

"How did you get down here, Mrs. Sacks?" Lambert asked.

"He—He heard you," she said. "He got off the bed and grabbed his clothes. I ran. H-He has a gun!"

Lambert looked at Clint, silently asking if he believed her. Clint shook his head, but the sheriff couldn't be sure. He drew his gun.

"Sheriff—" Clint said.

"Stay here with her, Adams," he said. "I'll go upstairs."

"No, wait—"

He started to move, but Julia held him tightly. He realized she wasn't clinging to him, she was holding him prisoner.

"Julia, let go!"

"Don't leave me!"

Lambert moved toward the stairs, just as Frank Burkett appeared at the top, wearing jeans, but barefoot and shirtless. And with a gun in his hand.

"Look out!" Julia shouted.

Burkett heard voices downstairs, but didn't understand them. He started down from the top when the sheriff appeared, and then he heard Julia shout. His gun was in his hand, so he lifted it . . .

The sheriff saw Burkett bringing his gun up.

"Hold it!" Lambert shouted, but knew he was too late.

Burkett fired. The bullet struck the sheriff high on the

right side, dropping him. Burkett started down the steps the rest of the way.

At the sound of the shot, Clint forcefully pushed Julia away. She struck the sofa, which overturned.

Clint rushed to the hallway as Burkett came down the stairs with his gun held out. He turned and brought the gun to bear on Clint.

"Stop!" Clint shouted, knowing this was wrong. Julia had set this man up to be killed, and by the look on Burkett's face, there was no way he could stop it.

He fired.

FORTY-FIVE

Clint checked Burkett's body.

"Is he dead?" Julia asked.

Clint didn't answer. He went to the sheriff, sat him up so he could check his wound.

"I'm okay," Lambert said, "but damn, it hurts."

"I'll get you to the doctor," Clint said.

"Is Burkett dead?"

"Yes."

"And Mrs. Sacks?"

"She set this up, Sheriff," Clint said. "Took the man to bed, left him up there to come down and tell us he raped her, so we'd kill him when he came down. She's devious."

"Clint—"

"Take it easy."

"No, Clint," Lambert said. "Behind you."

Clint turned, saw Julia standing there holding a small-caliber gun on them.

* * *

Julia didn't know who to shoot first, the law or Clint Adams. But Sheriff Lambert was already on the floor, bleeding from a wound, so she turned her gun on Clint.

"You men," she said, "you're all so easy."

Clint knew she was going to shoot, and he had holstered his gun.

"Julia," he said, "Jerry is still alive."

She froze.

"You're lying."

"No, I'm not," he said. "They took him to the doctor's office and found a heartbeat. Of course, he might be dead by now, but if he isn't, then you'd be committing murder for nothing now."

"The bitch, I shot the bitch."

"She's alive, too," Clint said.

She looked at Lambert.

"He's lying, isn't he?"

"No," Lambert said through the pain, "he's tellin' the truth. Right now you're not guilty of anything. We can't even get you for settin' up poor Frank here, because we can't prove it."

Clint was straightening up slowly, getting himself into position where he could draw and fire before she could fire—if he was fast enough.

Julia was considering what they were telling her, then firmed her jaw and said, "I'll have to take the chance."

So would Clint.

He drew . . .

FORTY-SIX

Clint checked out of the hotel and walked out onto the boardwalk. He had, indeed, been lying to Julia. Jerry Sacks was dead. Frank Burkett was dead. Julia was dead. The only one who had survived her wounds was Antonia, who also had her prize money.

Before checking out, he had stopped at her room to check on her. It had been three days since she'd been shot. The bullet had missed her heart, and the doctor had been able to extract it . . .

"Still hurts like hell," she told him.

"It will for a while," he said.

"You should know," she said. "How many times have you been shot?"

"I lost count."

"I don't know how you do it," she said. "Once is enough for me. I better not be too stiff to shoot properly."

"You've got enough money to retire from pool," he said.

"Then what would I do?"

"Travel? Live?"

"Travel sounds good, but I think I'll go where they have pool tables."

"Suit yourself."

"You leaving?" she asked.

"Right now."

"I'm sorry about your friend."

"So am I," he said. "In the future I think I'll stick to poker."

"Good," she said. "I don't want to have to play against you again. Don't know that I'd be able to keep you from the table."

"You won't have to worry about that."

He leaned over and kissed her. She grabbed the front of his shirt and held him tightly.

"I wish we had more time together," she said.

"So do I," he said, but not enough to stay. He was done with Tucson . . .

As Clint was walking to the livery, he decided to stop at the sheriff's office. Lambert was behind his desk, his arm in a sling. Clint had never met his deputy, but knew the man was out doing rounds. Maybe Lambert had even hired a second man, until he was healed.

"Headin' out?" the lawman said.

"Yep, all done with this town," Clint said.

"Can't say I blame you," Lambert said. He stood up and extended his left hand for an awkward handshake. "That was a helluva move you pulled on Mrs. Sacks. I never saw anybody draw like that, while under the barrel."

"We gave her just enough to think about it," Clint said. "Thanks for going along with me."

"Figured it was the only way for us to come out alive," Lambert said. "Where you headed?"

"Not sure, but it'll be somewhere I can play poker, not pool."

"But I heard you were good at pool."

"Not my game," Clint said. "I wouldn't ever want to get beat again without having a chance to play. At least in poker everybody gets a fair shot. What's happening with the Sacks ranch?"

"I don't know," Lambert said. "The law will have to decide what happens to the property and the money. Far as I know, there ain't no family."

"Is there a will?"

Lambert shrugged.

"That's for lawyers to decide. Think you might be in the will?"

"I doubt it, but I'm not going to hang around to find out," Clint said. "If I am, give my share to the local church."

"You might have to sign off on that legally."

"If I have to, I will," Clint said. "It's time for me to get going."

"Well, watch your back."

"It's how I live my life, Sheriff," Clint said, and left.

Watch for

CHICAGO CONFIDENTIAL

347th novel in the exciting GUNSMITH series
from Jove

Coming in November!

And don't miss

**THE GUNSMITH:
ANDERSONVILLE VENGEANCE**

Gunsmith Giant Edition 2010

Available from Jove in November!

GIANT-SIZED ADVENTURE FROM AVENGING ANGEL LONGARM.

BY TABOR EVANS

2006 Giant Edition:

LONGARM AND THE OUTLAW EMPRESS

2007 Giant Edition:

LONGARM AND THE GOLDEN EAGLE SHOOT-OUT

2008 Giant Edition:

LONGARM AND THE VALLEY OF SKULLS

2009 Giant Edition:

LONGARM AND THE LONE STAR TRACKDOWN

2010 Giant Edition:

LONGARM AND THE RAILROAD WAR

penguin.com/actionwesterns

M456AS0510

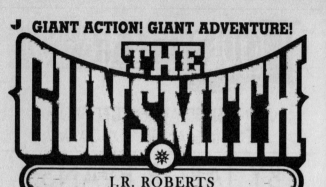

GIANT ACTION! GIANT ADVENTURE!

THE GUNSMITH

J.R. ROBERTS

DON'T MISS A YEAR OF

Slocum Giant
by
Jake Logan

Slocum Giant 2004:
Slocum in the Secret
Service

Slocum Giant 2005:
Slocum and the Larcenous
Lady

Slocum Giant 2006:
Slocum and the Hanging
Horse

Slocum Giant 2007:
Slocum and the Celestial
Bones

Slocum Giant 2008:
Slocum and the Town
Killers

Slocum Giant 2009:
Slocum's Great
Race

Slocum Giant 2010:
Slocum Along
Rotten Row